THE SKI BUM

HARPER & ROW, PUBLISHERS

NEW YORK AND EVANSTON

THE SKI BUM

ROMAIN GARY

THE SKI BUM

1

THERE WAS IZZY BEN ZWI, WHO HAD ONCE SPENT
twenty-five days on his skis in the Andes, at seventeen
thousand feet, where no one ever saw a pair of skis before,
or anything else for that matter, the first man to make a
run down the slopes of the First Cordillera, where the
Pula Indians had settled centuries ago, fleeing away from
whoever it was that exterminated them: there is always
someone around; they had settled there because no Spaniard
was able to breathe that high, and so they could have their
normal life span of thirty years run out its course quietly.
A bad, clumsy, straight-line skier, whose eyes had the
quiet, hungry look of one who lives only for the something that isn't there, and who is driven higher and higher
each year by everything that *is* there all right; he was
bound to end up one day like the Englishman John Reeves,
whom they found in the Himalayas frozen on his skis,
fifteen years after he had disappeared in the Ebor Mountains. Escape artists. They all knew that Izzy had it in
him: he was the kind of ski bum they call *fada* in the
French Alps, meaning a nut, despised by the real pros,

the way the wild skier is always despised by technicians. He came from a kibbutz in Israel and had never seen snow until he was twenty-five years old, but then it was love at first sight. Lenny never cared much for him; there was just too much seriousness in him, something almost religious, and the way he talked about snow, shyly, earnestly, haltingly, made you uneasy and suspicious. It's all right, you felt like telling him, it's only snow, don't make too much of it, don't make it sound so damn important, leave it alone, it's good enough as it is. Words. You can make words of almost anything. Vocabulary sets in and then the next thing you know you'll find yourself thinking. A big, heavy, blond Jew, whose family had been butchered by the Germans during the war, which was all right as long as one didn't make a chronic sickness out of it, as if there was not enough bloody psychology in the world anyway. There was Alec Jeannot, a Frenchman from Chamonix, probably the best slalom expert among the Alpine Guides, who had been only a technician until he discovered that his wife was sleeping with somebody or other, and that made him a real snow lover, as the pros call them, they usually spit after they say it, and it was true that Jeannot got on your nerves more often than not because he was looking at the snapshots of his children all the time, trying to figure out the likeness and to remember the faces of all the clients he had taken climbing in summer. Lenny couldn't understand why he cared so deeply, it was just one of those things, the world was made of them. He would spread the snapshots on the table in Bug Moran's chalet, two boys, one girl, brooding over them. None of the kids looked in the least like him.

– For Chrissakes, Lenny told him, forget about this demography business.

– I think the elder boy looks a little like me.

– Yeah.

You couldn't even get rid of him by putting your skis on and going for a good run. There was nowhere to go. No snow. It was summer. There was no getting away from it. They were stranded in Bug Moran's chalet on the rocks like fish on the sand. Summer. The worst thing that can hit a guy. Some bums were teaching water skiing on the lake in Geneva, on the Costa Brava or on the Riviera, but they hated water skiing, all of them. They hated that rope business. You were never on your own. Always dragging along in tow. There was Stanko Zavitch, from Yugoslavia, twice winner of the Sokol Award in his land, who took bigger risks on his skis than anyone Lenny had ever seen before, and thought nothing of going full speed through the fir-tree forest at Ognen, three miles of thickly growing trees, at a thousand francs a time, to get enough money to keep his two brothers studying at the Polytechnikum in Zürich, and who ended by breaking his neck all right, but one of the brothers had completed his studies by then and was taking care of the other, so it was not too bad. He could still ski, though, but of course he was limited in his body movements, and had had to develop a strange, jerky style of his own, not being able to bend his back; he couldn't walk uphill, and they had to pull him over the Berthold to reach the top where Bug Moran's chalet was, and where they could eat, drink and sleep free during the summer months. They all knew that Bug was a queer but he never made you feel his problem. He never went beyond staring at you with his big, dumb, meaningful eyes, like a huge St. Bernard dog who got it all wrong and was sitting there on his behind, waiting to be rescued. You didn't have to rescue him, so it was all right. He was much better than some of the fellows who came up to you for skiing lessons and took it for granted that you were available. It was hard to make a living up there, even at the peak of the season: the Swiss pros were a tightly knit group, they had a union too, you were supposed to be a tourist there and not permitted to teach skiing, and the bums had to do it on the side, at cut rates, and when some of the wives tipped you too well you could always play dumb and pretend you didn't know at all what was on their minds. During his whole two seasons in Switzerland, Lenny had managed most of the time to ignore what they had on their minds and still eat and have at least three days a week of clean snow all to himself. It was rough, but then it was what life was about anyway. The local *Ski Lehrers* hated their guts: the bums were always better looking, they took bigger risks, they had more glamour, there was an air of adventure about them and so it was hard on the Swiss, naturally. Once or twice, usually on Sundays, some of the bums got beat up by the local guys, some were asked to leave by the authorities as "undesirable aliens without visible means of support." And when Ed Storyk from Wyoming got buried under an avalanche, while skiing in the *verboten* area of the Helmutt glacier, the bums had been hounded off the slopes mercilessly for two weeks, and the local press warned the tourists against the "irresponsible, inexperienced, self-styled skiing instructors who ignored the elementary rules of safety." But then business always picked up in the end: they were by far the best-looking bunch of men around.

And they were all in Bug Moran's chalet now, bracing themselves for the summer. There was Bernard Peel, the Earl, as they called him, a lean, haunted-looking Englishman, who had learned to ski when he was a TB patient in Davos, two years ago, and who had never been below five thousand feet since. You never saw him except in summer. When the snow was good he disappeared completely, out of sight, there was no way of telling if it was a bloody lie or if it was true, as even some of the Swiss guides claimed, that he had crossed on skis the forty-three-mile stretch between Mount Valli and the Stück in the Oberland, where even the famous Mossens brothers lost their lives in 1946. That's how a legend is built: by not being seen. That's how God struck it so big. You always end up by thinking about God, up there. It's got to have something to do with altitude. Heights. Peaks. Sometimes a guy just can't help thinking. That's the trouble with being a ski bum in summer. Thought-shit sets in. Every year, the Earl's father, a marquis or a duke, some kind of bastard anyway, would come from his castle in England and plead with his son to come back home, and the Earl would stand there in his crazy blue Bersagliere hat, his red sweater and green pants, listening to the voice of his blood and hearing nothing. They called him *Heilig* in the Oberland, a nickname that went back to the legend of Grütli, who was supposed to have been the first man to walk on skis and who was worshiped as a saint by the Swiss Tourist Office. None of them spoke any French or Schweizerdeutsch, except the Earl, who could speak in five languages to no one. The most silent son of a bitch you could find, and there was more hostility in him than in anyone Lenny had ever met, which was a remarkable thing for a guy who had only one lung. You couldn't help liking him. Not speaking the language was the best thing about Switzerland. You were safe there. Back home, the language problem was everywhere. Anyone could come up and talk to you, try their friendliness on you. People always liked him, he had the kind of blond good looks that made every woman feel protective or worse, and as there was no language barrier there was very little you could do about it. He did a couple of seasons as a skiing instructor in Sun Valley and it was like one great big happy family out there. They really made you feel you belonged, that you were one of them. It scared the shit out of him. Everything is always much easier when you don't speak the language. You don't have to be rude to people. You don't have to tell them: No thanks, I don't want to go and stay with you in Miami, I have no use for anything that lies below six thousand feet, and that includes you. None of the bums cared a damn what they did when there was no snow. Some even went to work, or got married to some local girl with a nice behind and a steady job, who saw them through the critical summer months and then never saw them again. It simply didn't matter to a bum what he did below six thousand feet. The only thing that mattered was not to get trapped in the glue down there, like Ronnie Shahn, who went down to Zürich last May, out of sheer hunger, and they found him two months later in a stationery shop, selling pencils, married to a Swiss girl who was cooking for him. They never heard of him again. It couldn't have been hunger alone, the general opinion was that she had put something in his food. Lenny often wondered why so many ski bums were Americans, maybe because when you have a really big country behind you, you have got to run. You just don't want the responsibility. And it was a nice, comfortable thing to be a young American abroad, because you had the reputation of being dumb and inarticulate anyway, and what with the language barrier you were really safe there. All you had to do was to conform to their idea of the young, innocent American in Europe, and to turn on that typically American grin, standing in some street with your sleeping bag and your skis, and looking nice, handsome and lost, and even though the police knew you were a vagrant they would leave you alone. America could still do a lot of things for you, provided you left it far behind you. There is a lot to be said for prestige. And the nice thing about Europe is that they all have the American Dream over here. They all know for sure that even though you are arrested for sleeping in public places, railway stations or under a bridge, you're not a bum, without a franc in your pocket and no change of clothes, they think you're only a little crazy and looking for experience, they know you'll be back next year driving a Cadillac. And so that's how American prosperity keeps you going, no matter how broke you are.

– Bug, why is it they like Americans so much here? Bug was spread all over his couch, all two hundred pounds of him, gasping for breath: allergy. He was allergic to almost anything, most of all to himself.

– It's not that they like Americans here, Lenny. They just like you.

– What's wrong with me?

– There's something likable about your face, you bastard. You can't help that.

Bug's parents had built the chalet for him at almost nine thousand feet, because supposedly there was no asthma there. It must have been one of the most expensive jobs in Switzerland: every bit of wood or stone had to come up on sleighs. The chalet stood alone on a rock and the village of Wellen was a thousand feet below. You could see the Ebig and more snow than almost anywhere else in the world, except perhaps in the Himalayas. Everything was de luxe. Bathrooms, beds, crazy modern chairs, pink porcelain johns that made you feel guilty, you felt you were doing something awful to them. Bug Moran was rich. From time to time, though, after a bad relapse of pansies, he would go to Zürich and commit himself to a clinic there. Having Bug around was bad enough. But to make your summer really lousy he had brought up from Zürich two weeks ago some sort of a poet with two books published, and one of those open railway tickets for a whole year's travel in Europe on as many trains as you wish, that you could purchase at cut rates, in dollars. And so the bastard got somehow to Zürich without quite knowing how or why, simply by changing trains all the time, and Bug had met him in the men's room of the Zürich railway station, where he went regularly, and they began to talk poetry there, and it all ended up with Bug bringing the guy up the mountain, to the chalet. And now the talk that was going on in the chalet was simply goddamn awful, with Genghis Cohn—that was the guy's name— reciting poetry at them and telling them that they were lost and unacquainted with the truth. And you had to take it all, at Bug Moran's, it was all part of your meal ticket.

– The trouble with you guys is that you live for your-selves. Personal happiness—well, I simply do not accept this sort of obligation. I say: happiness is strictly for others. You must realize that you are born free and there is abso-lutely no obligation for you to be happy. Personally, I may add, I have always had a death wish and I'm not a bit ashamed of it. Death is renewal. Death is fertility. It makes things grow. All the great things in life start in death. Death alone makes for great literature. What American literature has always lacked, with the possible exception of Edgar Poe, is corruption, rot, decay, death. A real cultural achievement is always a form of decay. Look at Baudelaire, Rimbaud, Proust, Genet, Dostoevski. Rotten to the core, all of them, and look what they have given to the world. But it is a slow process, of course. You can't get rotten immediately. It takes time. But America is still a young country and we can make it.

He was a little guy and looking at him one would never guess there was room for so much horseshit in him. It went on and on until the small hours of the morning and sometimes the bums felt they were paying too much for food and shelter. And they also had to listen to some crazy jazz and poetry records by Mischa Boubentz, Arch Metal, Stan Gavelka, Jerry Lasota, Dick Brillianski, or then Genghis Cohn would read aloud pages of his own Spiritual Achievement. It was really more than you could eat in one day, no matter how hungry you were, and so Lenny would put on his skis and glide slowly among the stars until dawn, when the first bells of Wellen's milk dogs were heard in the valley below. There was a time not so long ago when he could go and spend the night with Tilly, the barmaid of the Linden Hotel, blonde, soft and so full of glue it almost ruined sex for him. You must never feel too sure of yourself and imagine that there's no danger around. Emotions. Love. Tenderness. Life propaganda, that's what it was. You had to watch it all the time. You fall for that and then life goes important on you. Some of the most experienced bums got caught in the glue and were never heard of again. For the first few weeks everything had been fine between Tilly and him, some of the best sex he had ever had, although you could smell trouble by the way she caressed his hair and gazed into his eyes lovingly. Tilly spoke only French and Schweizerdeutsch and Lenny spoke neither, and so, what with the language barrier between them, it was about as perfect a human relationship as you could hope for. But then Tilly played a dirty trick on him. She bought some damn Linguaphone records, studying secretly, and before he knew what hit him she was speaking English at him just like that, straight from the hip, in a funny, sweet, singsong voice, and soon it was yes, Tilly, I love you too, I sure do, you're a marvelous girl, Tilly, yes, yes, I know you would do anything for me, now excuse me, it's so hot in this room, I have a fellow waiting for his lesson down there, see you soon, sure, sure. There'll never be anyone but you in my life, but I have to run now. She was even beginning to talk about America in a meaningful sort of way, and how she could find a job there and did he think his parents would like her, and so he found himself explaining things to her, I have no parents, my father was in the army and got himself killed, my mother has married and remarried until I lost track of her, I'm a bum, a ski bum, all I care about is snow, that is, except you, of course. Yes, I know you can cook. Yes, I know I can break my neck going on the *verboten* track and the Kleine Scheidegg, but I like it there, there's no one around, I don't want to have children, I love my children so much already that I don't want to give them a father like myself, it would be a dirty trick to play on them. The fellow who invented the Lingua-phone records was one of the most truly vicious fiends who had ever lived, breaking the language barrier and poisoning the fine, simple, safe, human relationship he had with Tilly. A regular home wrecker. So one day he simply didn't go back to her, even though it had meant a lot to him at the time, it meant going hungry, and when she came to see him on the slopes while he was teaching he had to tell her that it was all over between them, be-cause there was a limit to what he could take from love.

– But why, Lenny? Why? I love you deeply, truly and forever.

– I never saw anybody learn to speak a language quicker and better than you, Tilly. Honest. That Linguaphone bastard must be a genius. I can't tell you why, Tilly. I don't like to talk. I don't even speak to myself. Got nothing to say. I haven't been on speaking terms with myself for years, Tilly.

– What have I done?

– Listen, we had a fine working relationship. But now it's becoming personal.

– I don't understand you, Lenny.

– Please don't cry, Tilly. People will think you're in love with me.

– But I am in love with you, Lenny. I never loved anyone more in my life.

– Look, my mother fell in love with a man when I was fifteen and what's become of her? I don't know. That's what's become of her.

– Lenny . . .

– I wish you'd stop crying, Tilly. It's bad for business. Nobody's going to hire me if they think I'm already taken. When they hire a ski instructor they like to be sure he's available.

– You can have all the women you must have, I don't care. I know that a man's work comes first.

– They won't get it from me, you know that. It's just that they like to imagine they can. Anyway, I don't like to talk about it. I just hate hurting anyone, I don't even like to hurt myself.

He had missed Tilly's comforting, sheltering body for a few days, and somehow he had felt the cold more than usually, but there was almost nothing in the world he couldn't get rid of when he had his skis on, and he had a good break, a German couple with three kids, who had hired him for the season, and after they left he went on a trek from Wellen to Broye in the Grisons, sleeping in the shepherds' summer huts, except one night on the Benni Range, when he couldn't find the hut buried under the snow, and although he was probably as resistant to cold as a loner can be, he almost froze to death before reaching, at dawn, the Mount Benni Refuge, where a kind, heavily bearded lawyer from Lyon shared his can of cassoulet with him, the greatest break he had ever had in his life. A wise, round, bald man, with tortoiseshell glasses, who took one look at him as he staggered in, and pushed the can with the steaming cassoulet and sausage and duck meat among white beans toward him, and it was almost incredible that the world should have so much to offer. The lawyer talked to him knowingly about America, where he had never been. You could always have it both ways in Europe: they either liked the U.S.A. and so were delighted to feed you, or else they felt superior, scornful and spiteful about America, and "everything it stood for," and so they were even more delighted to feed you and patronize you, it made them feel even more scornful and superior. Unfortunately, though, the lawyer spoke good English and so Lenny had the nasty feeling he was making him pay for his meal.

– A quarter of the American population is between twelve and twenty years old, the Frenchman explained to him. The expanding universe . . . *Alors,* what happens? Three summers ago I was climbing the Hornbnutt with a guide. It's a rough climb. They've broken it down the last year, so now almost anybody can make it with a guide, but that was before. At about eight thousand feet there is a small cave, and inside we found a young American, half dead. He couldn't get any higher and he couldn't get down.

Well, I suppose it's a big, powerful country, and it's not easy to get away from things.

Jesus Christ, Lenny thought, here we go again. Psychology. Sociology. Insight. Show me yours and I'll show you mine. They are after you all the time. A few months earlier, he had been making love to a French girl in a chalet at Wengen, and the mother caught him in the morning, as he was trying to slip out quietly, tucking his shirt in and holding his shoes in his hand. There was no good denying anything, so he tried desperately to find something nice to say in French, and he finally came up with *merci beaucoup,* almost the only words he knew then, but it was not the right thing to say at all, apparently, in the circumstances, but then it was too late, the mother began to scream, and he didn't know how to get out of this fix, but managed at least not to say *à votre santé,* which was the only other sentence he knew in French, and just stood there, grinning, American, very pleasant and everything, until the woman got even more furious and called her husband. Now, it seems something was happening in Cuba then, some sort of war was being called off, although Lenny really didn't know a damn thing about it and didn't care. He stood on the staircase sheepishly, holding his shoes, the father came out in his pajamas, a worried little man with a mustache, an Armenian-looking sort of Frenchman, and his wife proceeded to tell him everything, and the girl came out too, crying and behaving as if she had never done anything like that before, which was definitely and deliciously untrue, and Lenny struggled for some French words that weren't there to find, something nice to say about General de Gaulle or Albert Schweitzer, looking for some firm, common ground on which to meet a proud ally under difficult circumstances. His shirt was still smudged all over with lipstick and although he had his pants on he didn't look at all convincing, and finally the father, after a good look at him, asked in a grave, meaningful voice:

– You are American?

– Yes, sir, Lenny said, wishing they would stop making politics out of everything.

The man leaned toward him:

– Do you think there is going to be a war between the United States and Soviet Russia, because of these launching sites in Cuba?

There were moments like this when Lenny was so scared by the sheer crazy unpredictability of human beings that he got goose pimples. For all their familiar noses, mouths, hands, they were really almost mythical creatures from another planet. It was the funniest thing. He simply didn't know what to make of them. There was more to them than he cared to think about. Even their mortality wasn't a bit reassuring; they died, yes, but it wasn't that simple, he still felt that even then there was more trouble lurking somewhere. You had to laugh, that was all you could do and it wasn't much. They were dangerous. They were dangerous because you could easily fall for them, and then you were in the glue all right. They could get you sub-

liminal, sort of. You had to watch out all the time. It
was not enough to be tough and cynical, it was an old
trick and everybody could see through it, and even though
he considered himself one of the world's finest liars, the
only time when he felt safe and out of reach was when
he was crossing some white, virgin nothingness on his skis.
But you couldn't spend your life skiing, so you had to lie a
lot. There was only one man to whom he had almost told
the truth about himself, and that was Ernst Fabricius, in
Davos Sanatorium, where the great old skier of the Emile
Allais days lay dying, his lungs eaten away. Lenny had put
on his skis and had gone to see him all the way from
Wellen, when the rumor reached the bums at the chalet
that Ernst was sinking and they had drawn lots to decide
who would carry the *Grütli* to him, the small wooden doll
that was still made by the peasants in the village where
the first skier was born. Lenny hated the whole damn
sentimental crap of it, it was pure horseshit anyway, the
Grütli Stück was an invention of the Swiss Tourist Bureau,
but it was Bug Moran's decision and it was late May and
Bug and his chalet were becoming important. They drew
lots and of course it fell on him and he had to carry the
grinning puppet up to Davos and put it on Ernst's bed.
As he sat there the rage at the whole damn, cheap situation
hit him so hard he had to make a good clean sweep of it.
He could lie his way out of almost anything human.

– Ernst, could I borrow a hundred francs from you? I'll
pay it back someday. Honest.

It was a good try but it failed. Fabricius raised his head a little and smiled.

– You don't have to reassure me, sonny. I know what I'm in for. Thanks all the same.

– Ernst, I'm only trying to borrow some dough. Come on, be human. A hundred francs. I'll pay you back next month.

Emotions. He was trying hard to get rid of the glue. He knew his face was okay. Cynical.

– The head nurse told me you're due any day now. Did they tell you? I bet they didn't. I bet they make all sorts of reassuring sounds, eh?

– Sure they do. They don't know about bums like us, Lenny. They think we like it here.

– Could I take your boots, Ernst? They are just my size.

– Sure, take them.

– Thanks. It's good to get away from boots and things at last, eh Ernst? How does it feel?

– Great.

– You must be about forty years old. You've got experience. Did it ever make sense to you? Did you ever feel happy? Aside from skiing, I mean?

– No, Lenny, I've managed to avoid that. That's why I feel okay now.

– I suppose there's something in that oriental crap. Stoicism.

– That's not oriental, Lenny. It's Greek.

– Well, whatever it is. Like skiing. I don't like the deal

we're given. You can't get anything here you aren't going to lose. Mortality. The terms are laid down for you, like it or not. Fucking democracy.

– How are the bums?

– The summer's coming down there, so you aren't missing much. Butterflies. There was some talk about holding up a bank in Zürich. Plenty of banks down there. But then it takes weeks of preparation and you may as well go into the banking business. Who pays for the clinic, anyway?

– Some Austrian people here. They say I gave them skiing lessons in Kitzbühel years ago. I don't remember them at all. Rich people are funny. Philanthropy.

– What's that?

– Feeling good.

– Do you have any folks back home? I mean, somebody to notify?

– Nobody that's worth wasting a good stamp on, Lenny.

– Ernst.

– Yes?

– What's it all about?

– I don't know, kid. I enjoyed some of it, though.

He hung around Davos until the old man died two weeks later and then skied around awhile looking for him, sort of. He went down the Gruhn Tahl Forest, down the Sturm and all the way to the Aarberg, wondering sometimes how far you could go nowhere. He had taken Ernst's beautiful thermos flask marked "U.S. Army property," which gave him a kick because they had called him up several times for military service, little bits of official papers reaching him now and then, as if to remind him that he truly existed. You always leave a mark, no matter what. A blonde Swiss-Deutsch girl took a snapshot of him as he stood in a street in Davos trying to figure out how to steal the two yards of sausage hanging just behind the door of a delicatessen shop; and then the girl came up to talk to him and he knew at once that he would get the sausage with a little courtesy.

– Where are you from?

– Montana, U.S.A.

It wasn't true, but lying was a matter of principle with him. You have to cover up your tracks, no matter what.

– You are on the American Olympic team?

– No, I'm a no team. I'm a loner.

– What's that?

– I don't go for group activities. Would you know anyone around here who needs skiing lessons?

– I do. I cannot pay much.

– You don't have to pay anything. You buy us that strip of sausage hanging there, and I'll give you eight days' lessons for free.

She was a secretary from Basel on a two-week vacation and the two-week limit suited him fine. He should have known, however, from past experience, that it was a lousy start for a good romantic relationship to be picked up by a girl, hungry, in the street of a skiing resort; it made them feel they were onto a good thing and then you soon found yourself answering sad, monotonous little questions and you had to lie to them like a gentleman, if you didn't want to hurt them, with your brains turning inside out in desperation, and there is simply no sausage in the world that is worth the effort.

– I do, Trudi, honest I do. I've never been so much in love before. That's why we must leave each other, while it's still beautiful. No good trying to make things last, Trudi, it's inhuman.

– But we could live happy forever, together, *Schatzchen*. I could find you a job in Zürich, in a travel agency.

– Now, don't say things like that to me, Trudi. Please don't.

– You don't love me.

– Listen, Trudi, when people love each other the way we do, they must preserve the memory of it.

– But we can be . . .

He tried to make love to her, to take her mind off it, but then it caught up with her again as soon as he had finished. She was full of glue and she had that placid, firm Swiss obstinacy that could drive you nuts and it was a terrible thing the way the whole world spoke English now, a fellow had nowhere to go.

– Trudi, when two people begin to stick together for good they end up by having jobs, kids, homes, cars, problems, and that's no love no longer, that's living. We don't want that.

–We don't have to get married, Lenny, if you don't wish to. I understand about principles. I could take care of your child without being married.

Outer Mongolia, he thought suddenly. There was a place somewhere called Outer Mongolia.

–Please, Trudi. You must help me. I love to regret things. That's my nature. I'll regret you so much, honey, you'll be like a queen, sitting there on the throne of my memory. . . .

Holy Moses, he thought, where do I get all this crap from? Why don't I just grab my skis and run? There's no point in lying to her anyway, she doesn't appreciate it. I've simply got to learn how to hurt people, that's what honesty is about. Two, three weeks, that was about as far as lying could take him, beyond that he just couldn't deliver, honesty was setting in. He was getting angry now, spring was coming and you had to go higher and higher for snow, where there were no tourists and no way to make a living, and then you find a nice, warm, comfortable girl and she turns out to be mean and wants to marry you.

–I'll take good care of you, Lenny.

–Where did you learn such good English, Trudi?

–At the Basel Berlitz School.

–You ought to try Chinese next. It's a beautiful language, I hear, and they say it's got a great future.

But he didn't want to hurt her, you have to care deeply about people to wish to hurt them, and so he touched her hand gently and talked to her with sweet, dumb Berlitz talk, that was why she had paid five hundred francs for a three-month tuition course in Basel, dreaming of a tall, handsome American she would meet one day on the ski slopes, and he felt he was included in the guarantee and that the Berlitz people were watching him, and the bums later told him he was a fool, with his good American looks he should have gone to the Berlitz people long ago and asked them for a cut. People were making money on your back all the time. Hell, I'm going to sue them, he thought. He knew that hurting a woman only brings her closer to you and the more she feels rejected the more she becomes sure that she is living the greatest love of her life, and as the great Persian poet Don Zysskind once said, the great Zysskind who was given a moth- and bug-eaten carpet by the Shah of Persia for immortal poetry he had written, as the great Zysskind had expressed it in his *tokhes,* which is the Persian form of those Japanese pearls of wisdom called *hokusai* or *sukiyaki*: "Watch it, man, you kick a woman twice without actually meaning anything and the next thing you know you've started a relationship." And there was another famous *sukiyaki* or *harakiri* by the same Zysskind, very popular among the bums, which ran:

> *You must never kill your brother.*
> *Why bother?*

Zysskind was making a good living in summer selling his beautiful Japanese or Persian pearls of wisdom to Chinese restaurants for rice cookies, but then he went into the Chinese cooking business himself, explaining that he wanted to be his own publisher, married a half-Negro half-

Chinese waitress who gave him three children, all by the same man, and so he was back in the Bug Moran chalet, and Lenny liked him, although he rather avoided having Jewish friends because since they had been exterminated by Hitler they always brought their dead family around, and some of them took up skiing for the wrong reasons, escape artists, all of them. There is something mysterious about people's capacity for suffering, they are really very creative there. In the beginning he kept telling Don to stop brooding about it, suppose you had a loving wife and three kiddies all your own, you would never be able to get out of that mess, but there was no logic in the fellow, only a capacity for suffering. So he took the guy with him on a good ski run through the Thal, over the Ebbert, and down the hills and they spent the night in a chalet Lenny knew, a rich diamond merchant from Amsterdam owned it and was away all the time, and they broke in and slept there in real beds and then went on to Grisons and then, a week later, skied slowly down the Gründen at night, with the snow blue with moon and with the moon's eunuch face looking at them. Zysskind got inspired again and produced his most famous *hokusai*: "It's a beautiful world, as long as you can get away from it." But he couldn't get the message across to Trudi, she didn't go for oriental pearls of wisdom and it was all Greek to her. He could almost see himself sitting in a cozy little Schweizerdeutsch cottage with little heart-shaped Schweizerdeutsch windows, with a nice, small Schweizerdeutsch vegetable garden, and he was playing

with his lovely fair-haired Schweizerdeutsch daughter while
Trudi was singing gaily Schweizerdeutsch songs in the
kitchen and there would be a good Schweizerdeutsch dog
staring at him longingly and there would be a mailbox outside with his name and house number on it, and he felt his
hair stand on end. An address, an identity: the worst thing
that can hit a guy. Then they'd really know where to find
you. She got him so scared he jumped out of bed and
grabbed his pants, but it all turned out for the best, his
self-preservation instinct got kicked in the ass and went to
work and came up with a big, beautiful thing:

– Listen, Trudi, I've got to leave you. I'm a murderer.
The police are after me. Got to keep moving all the time.
Shot and killed a cop in Basel two months ago. Remember?
It was in the papers. I don't want to involve you in this,
Trudi, I don't want to ruin you. I don't want our children
to know their father was a compulsive killer.

It went down very well. She'd seen it all in the movies
before. America. They sure know about us in Europe. It
scared her so much she drew her blanket over her bare
behind. Protecting herself already. Sensitive bitch.

– *Mein Gott,* Lenny, why did you kill him?

– You don't have to have a reason to kill a man, Trudi.
It was nothing personal. I suppose the cop was a father
image to me. Authority. I'm mentally sick, Trudi. I've got
hostility.

He was putting his pants on quickly as he spoke,
trying to work up a mad, dark gleam in his eyes, while for

some reason that he couldn't fathom Trudi was pulling her blanket under her chin, now what the hell, he thought, why would she do that suddenly, protecting her bare ass just because I mentioned the police, some logic.

– I'll say goodbye now, Trudi. I'll be calling you from time to time. Wherever I am, no matter what happens to me, come hell or high water, I'll be thinking of you, maybe one day I'll be thinking of you, maybe one day I'll crawl bleeding and dying into your home and barricade myself in there and fight it out with the police to the last bullet, they aren't going to get us alive, Trudi, and maybe if you still love me you'll be reloading my gun for me. . . .

You can't go wrong in Europe if you make it really corny, they all know about America, the old country never lets you down. She just stared and stared at him with her big eyes full of horror, the American Dream, they all have it in Europe, it was no good upsetting things for the natives, one had to preserve their beliefs. But he thought better of it, you could make it too romantic and then she would really fall for him. You've got to have a sense of proportion. So he just walked out. The trouble was he didn't know the Swiss well enough. The next morning, as he was walking in Zermatt, trying to find Abe Sloninski, from Pittsburgh, who had lost faith two years ago and given up skiing and opened a small espresso coffee shop behind the Müller Hotel, called "Ye Olde Albert Einstein Memorial Espresso Coffee Shop and Hamburger," which was also a poetry workshop and local HQ for the Ban-the-Bomb Nuclear

Disarmament Committee and for the United-in-Peace Movement, and where an old-timer could always have a free
meal, two cops stopped him and before he knew it he was
under arrest in the Zermatt police station, trying to explain
that he had never killed anyone in Basel or anywhere else,
he was only trying to be nice to a girl who loved him
dearly and leave her without hurting her, love is a many-
splendored thing, no question about that. Gee, he thought,
it couldn't have taken her more than five minutes after
he left to grab the phone and notify the police, she sure
was one of the most honest and sincere girls he had ever
met, now, what was the vocabulary for it? There is always
a vocabulary for everything, yes, she had a conscience, that's
it, she had a conscience and purity, no wonder the Swiss
had the best watch industry in the world, they put into the
making of their clocks the best thing they've got in themselves: reliability.

– You have admitted to a witness that you shot and
killed a policeman, Karl Bohn, in Basel, three months ago.

– It was only kindness to animals, sir. I mean, I truly
said that to her, but I was only trying to be nice to her.

– The witness also says you have taken money from her.
That you have stolen money from her.

– No, sir. She's just in love with me, so she tries to hurt
me, that's what it is. I'm sure you know about love, sir, as
a policeman, I mean. It's murder.

The officer looked at him, trying to resist it, but then he
began grinning himself.

– We had a nice relationship, sir, but then love set in, and then of course everything went *kaputt*.

– You have a working permit? You have been giving skiing lessons here.

– I don't work, sir, only bumming around.

– What's that?

– That means being a tourist, sir.

– There seem to be quite a lot of young Americans like you in Switzerland. What keeps you here?

– Well, for one thing we love skiing. We love getting away from things. And then we don't speak the language. That's part of the fun.

He had left the police station with his spirits low, with the feeling that the world was becoming one big English-speaking place, and then they had noticed that his passport was out of date and told him to renew it or to leave the country, which he couldn't do, because he had the American Army on his back, a big powerful army, and if you told them you were a conscientious objector they would still put you to work, and still make you feel wanted and useful. It was a black day altogether. To make things worse the summer was all over you, the snow froze at night and turned soft and juicy in the morning, the rocks were showing everywhere, there was more and more earth around. Reality. It always caught up with you in the summer. There were almost no tourists around. The hotels were already closing for a month, getting ready for the climbing season; no more skiing lessons; some of the bums were giving up, washing dishes in the hotels at Wellen, talking about a passage back home on an army transport sailing from Amsterdam; some had a lucky break, like Johnny Lipski, who had been taken up by some intellectual French broad in Geneva, who loved the book he had written under the pen name of Tennessee Williams; Marty Stevens landed a job as a doorman in a Lausanne striptease joint, others just vanished into the clean blue air, never to be heard of again until their fat, bloated bodies would be found drifting through the corridors of New York offices, getting jobs, families, and dying happily ever after. There was only the hard core of the bums left at Bug Moran's chalet, the old-timers, where Bug himself was quarreling with a girl none of them had ever seen before, a little kid with a plain face and a good body, whom Bug found starving at the Zürich railway station. She had no money, she had lost her passport, she wanted to go to Rome and see Pope John XXIII because everybody had told her he was a nice man and it was worth it coming all the way from Indiana to see one, and Bug Moran found the kid an interesting bit of demography and brought her up with him. He was sitting now with his pipe stuck in his beard, pointing at the girl and discussing her in his dispassionate way that made her rather pleased with herself.

– A typical example of indiscriminate breeding, Bug was saying. Millions and millions of babies left to grow and then they go and call it America. Look at her. She hasn't got a clue. The enormous social implications of copulation are never seriously considered during the act. This girl shouldn't have been born at all. Just throwing babies around

won't do at all. You've got to organize some sort of welcome committee for them, damn it.

– That's creeping socialism, Genghis Cohn said.

– Listen, Bug, could you let me have fifty francs? Lenny
asked. I've got to go to Geneva, I've heard there's an opening
for me there. A chap called Angel called me up and left a
message with Müller's Hotel.

– Geneva? That's shit level.

– Well, I've got to eat.

– What sort of an opening?

– I don't know, Bug. I hardly know the fellow, he just
left a message saying he has something in my line.

– I didn't know you had a line, Lenny. What is it? Aside
from being very good-looking?

– I don't know, Bug. I think I could be very good on a
desert island or something.

Bug stared at him thoughtfully, sucking his pipe.

– Okay, Lenny, I'll give you the money, but answer a
philosophical riddle first.

– Aw, come off it.

– Who took the cookie from the cookie jar, Lenny?

– I don't know, Bug. Ask Pope John XXIII. Why pick
on me? That's thought-shit.

– Who took the cookie from the cookie jar?

– Keep your lousy fifty francs, Lenny said.

Bug gave him the money and Lenny went down to
Geneva.

2

THE MARMALADE DUCK'S NAME WAS LORD BYRON: HE
was lame. He was rich orange, with funny bits of hair
standing upright on his head, brown button eyes, and when
she picked him up he would always ask, *"Quoi? Quoi?"*
in French, and then settle down in her arms and go to sleep
and she would have to sit there for hours, holding him.
There were other ducks on the lake, seagulls, swans gliding
slowly like whips of Chantilly cream, and other black,
rather tough, proletarian-looking birds, and she came here
twice a day to feed them, it was her favorite spot in Geneva.
She was already putting in two days' work a week at the
local SPCA clinic, so she could say she had quite a full life,
really. You can't solve all the world's problems at once, you
have to begin somewhere.

There was only an hour to go before fetching her father
from the clinic and she still hadn't found the money to pay
the bill. She was also running out of gas. Nobody would
believe that the daughter of the American Consul in Geneva
had had no breakfast because she couldn't afford it, which
was actually as it should be: nobody should believe it. That

was what they were paid by State for: prestige. Prestige was an important element of American foreign policy and so to go hungry wearing a Chanel suit was the only patriotic thing to do. Her father had served his country so well that he had become a hopeless alcoholic in the process, in spite of his diplomatic immunity. Or perhaps because of it. Curious, this diplomatic immunity business. It keeps you so well protected that it can destroy you. Idealists should not be allowed to represent their country abroad, they can only take a limited amount of reality, preferably with gin. For the last few years his once promising career had been a steady climb down from one minor assignment to another; he was the sort of diplomat who simply couldn't see a man hanged and then put on his tuxedo and go to an official dinner with the executioners. This fatal streak in an American representative abroad was known in the Personnel Division book as "lack of emotional stability." He was a tall, handsome man, with kind, dark, humorous eyes, very elegant, very intelligent, but weak. There was no good denying that. She loved him very much, all the same.

She kissed Lord Byron goodbye, climbed up the stairs and into her little Sunbeam and drove off. She put Handel's *Messiah* on her record player with the vague hope of distracting her car's attention from its fuel problem. She knew that if even her old car let her down in the middle of town, she would simply burst out crying. There was a limit to what she could take from the facts of life. She hopefully raised the pitch of the *Messiah* full blast and somehow it worked: she did manage to reach the café. She had always known that her little Sunbeam was a sucker for music, or just a plain sucker, perhaps because it had lived with them long enough to be truly part of the family. As she stepped out of the car, a tall fellow with wild, blond hair and a pair of skis over his shoulder, who was leaning against the wall, grinned at her. American. She stared back at him coldly.

– What do those CC plates stand for?

– Consular Corps.

– What's that mean?

– That means I've got diplomatic immunity, okay?

He had to laugh, but she was inside the café already. Diplomatic immunity. I wouldn't be so sure if I were you, kid. He was glad she'd turned out to be so pretty, though, it made things much easier for him, you could do your best without forcing yourself. Some best. The minute you tried to live, you only got yourself into situations. But then it was summer, and the bare, hard earth was sticking out everywhere. No ski bum cares a damn what he does when he's below six thousand feet. It's all shit level down there and you've got to conform. He saw Angel emerge from the car parked across the street and walk toward him, lighting a cigarette. Black, narrow-brimmed camel's-hair hat, black suède shoes, black silk suit. Fancy bastard.

– That wasn't much of a shot.

– Get off my back, fellow, I don't need driving lessons, I've been on the road all my life. Why you always dressed

in black, anyway? So you don't have to change for your
funeral?

– Oh, *ça va.*

– You French?

– Algerian.

– Algerian? That's politics, eh? Well, beat it. I'm not
a dog. I need privacy. I can't get down to it, see, with your
eyes fixed on my ass. Can't work up enough conviction.
I've got to believe in what I'm doing. Or else I can't play
it natural.

– She wouldn't even talk to you.

– It's always like that with me. It hits them so hard
they've got to catch their breath.

He looked at the CC plates on the Sunbeam's tail.
Diplomatic immunity. That's what I'm up against. You
can't touch her. The kid doesn't look as if she truly had it,
though. Sensitive, kind of. Must hurt easy. You'll have to
do a lot of lying, Lenny, no point hurting her, she'll only
think it's love. Immunity, he thought, what d'you know.
That's about the best thing you can get down here. They
should give you a shot of it in the ass the minute you're
born.

3

THE LOUIS D'OR WAS A FAMOUS LANDMARK IN GENEVA,
very popular with the students, and the guidebooks mentioned it under the rubric *Intellectual Life.* The walls were
covered with photographs and portraits of some of the
most famous coffee drinkers who had lived in the city as
political exiles: Karl Marx, Kropotkin, Paderewski, and
there was even a snapshot of Lenin reading a newspaper
at the table where Chuck sat now, his nose stuck in Ma-
rengo's *Challenge of History,* which was required reading
this year at the University. He was a small, fragile-looking
Negro, the youngest son of a taxi driver from Birmingham.

– Listen, Chuck, could you let me have two hundred
francs?

– Why pick on me? You trying to be nice to us colored
folks?

– Chuck, everybody's on my back. The rent. The garage.
The butcher. It's a mess.

– Why don't you ask Paul? He's stinking rich.

– I can't borrow money from him, he's in love with me.
Ethics.

– I simply fail to understand how the daughter of an American Consul can be that broke. I would have thought we're paying enough taxes to keep you both in luxury.

– I don't know what they do with the taxpayers' money, Chuck, but I haven't had a new dress in six months.

– Here's a hundred francs, that's all I can do. I have eleven brothers and sisters slaving back home to keep me studying in Switzerland.

– That's okay, Chuck, I don't mind.

– Thanks.

He picked up his book again.

– By the way, the Pope seems to be a hell of a good guy, don't you think? You saw how he interrupted mass and made the priest take out that bit about the perfidious Jews? You know what, Jess? I would love to be elected Pope someday.

She looked at his nice Negro face and drew a deep breath.

– You've got to be an Italian to be elected Pope, she said tactfully.

She put a coin in the jukebox.

– I don't think I'll keep studying much longer, Chuck said. Escapism. Like all the kids are talking again about going to work on a kibbutz in Israel this summer. It's still the chic thing to do apparently. Last year, it was the Peace Festival in Moscow. The year before, building roads with the Youth Brigades in Yugoslavia. Last spring, the Ban-the-Bomb march in England. The young idealists' guide to

Europe. I think I'll go back to Birmingham and face things.

She was listening to a Bach fugue played by the Colin Sachs Jazz Trio.

– It's a beautiful arrangement, this jazz piece. The best trumpet I've heard since Chet Baker.

– You've heard they killed another civil rights leader back home?

She stood there for a moment, listening to the jukebox and then suddenly there were tears in her eyes and her lips twitched a little as she tried to smile.

– You know what, Chuck? I sometimes wish I were pregnant, just to have *something* to worry about. Be seeing you.

She went through the door to the bar, wishing it were her SPCA day, at least when you help a sick dog you feel less helpless yourself. The Birmingham race riots had upset her terribly. She still needed at least three hundred francs to pay some of the bills but there was no one she knew at the bar, except a Spanish ex-diplomat from prehistoric, pre-Franco days, who always talked about the Spanish civil war as if it still mattered, a former leader of the Rumanian social-democratic party, a former . . . Geneva was full of former people. The young man at the piano was playing a tune from *My Fair Lady,* but he should really have been playing Strindberg's Ghost Sonata. There used to be a time when they all had TB or idealism in Switzerland, except the Swiss, that is. Her father still had idealism, though it was 1963 and his first crack-up could be traced to the hanging of Stavrov in Bulgaria, in 1947: he had personally assured the Agrarian Liberals that the U.S.A., who were at that time members of the Allied Control Commission, would never allow the suppression of the democratic opposition. He had been given no instructions whatsoever to make such a commitment, he was merely acting out of deep understanding of everything his country stood for. Fatal.

Every American kid she knew, including herself, was now suffering from a disease the Germans called *Weltschmerz,* which is some kind of a world awareness, and this year they were talking about Pope John XXIII all the time. It used to be Ray Charles and Albert Schweitzer.

She had a big, explicit, striptease kind of body, that always made her self-conscious, and she had lived in too many countries and knew too little about too much. She did speak five languages fluently, though, plus some Hebrew and some Swahili, and for the last six months she had been working on a novel called *A Quality of Despair,* and that showgirl-type body of hers only added to the general confusion. The French students called her *une paumée,* meaning lost, only more so. She always had the best marks at the University, but her breasts always showed and the long legs and well-rounded hips didn't help a bit. She did feel all the time there was too much of her, both physically and emotionally.

Her mother had left them years ago, they were in Saudi Arabia then, and of course it was one of the best places in the world to leave from, daughter or no daughter. She was remarried to some car dealer back home now. Cadillacs. Jess always thought about her on Mother's Day, there is a soft spot in everyone.

A dark young man at the bar, with sharp, exotic features, was staring at her. She hated to be undressed in public. She ordered a Bloody Mary, which cost three francs, and she never touched alcohol, but the price included the delicious hors d'oeuvres at the counter, and her hand was on its way to the seventh salmon canapé. She simply *loved* eating. She hoped they didn't think she was hungry. It all had to be done in a very absent-minded and bored way because of American prestige abroad. She had had nothing substantial to eat since dinner at the Italian Consul-General's two nights ago. After dinner the Consul-General insisted on seeing her to her car and had tried to make love to her on the way down in the elevator. He lived on the second floor, too. What the hell did he think she was, instant coffee? The pianist was now playing a song from "Top Hat." God, how I love "Top Hat," and Fred Astaire. They were showing all those old pictures at the *ciné club* and it had been one of the greatest nonphilosophical experiences of her life. There were absolutely no problems in them. No reality. They were the greatest thing that had happened to the world since it developed gravity. One had to believe in something, dammit. She longed for a glass of milk, but this simply was not that sort of place. They had the biggest suicide rate in Switzerland, but then everybody had, the Swedes, the Danes, everybody. The fellow at the

bar was now trying to pick her up and she took her drink
and went over to the pianist, Eddie Weiss, a crew-cut, glassy
type from the West Coast. The American kids were all
over Europe now. *Weltschmerz.* They just ran blindly
around like young buffaloes.

– How're you, Ed?

– I don't know, Jess. I'm trying not to look. That guy
at the bar is sure interested in your behind. Keeps drilling.
In America it's breasts, but in Europe it's always your
ass that really matters. I wonder why?

– Well, it's a different culture.

She went to the powder room just to get out of that
fellow's range and recover her self-respect. Being a virgin
at the age of twenty-one didn't help, they all think it is
ready to snap. Perhaps the Peace Corps was the only solution, really. There was a limit to what working at the SPCA
could do for you.

When she came out she had a good break. François
was at the bar and she did pay him back the last time, she
was almost sure of it.

– François, I'm in a hurry, could you let me have five
hundred francs?

There was a man next to them at the bar, talking on the
phone.

– Well, I'm getting out. I don't trust the market, that's
why. Sell the Picasso, the Braques and the Dubuffet. Get me
some Delacroix and eighteenth century. Drawings, any-

thing. You can't go wrong with that. I'm sticking to the
blue chips for a while.

– How much did you say?

– Five hundred. I'll pay it back.

– Don't do that, but don't avoid me either. Here it is.
I'm still madly in love with you, you know.

– Don't say that, please, or I'll really have to give you
the money back.

– Did you hear that bit about Josette getting arrested?
One of the richest families in Geneva, and a member of a
call-girl ring. What the hell.

– Well, I suppose she wanted to be independent. I've got
to run now. Thanks again.

She went through the revolving door, turned right toward her car and ran smack into that grin again.

–Listen, you the American Consul here? The CC plate,
I mean? What's so funny? I'm in trouble. Broke. Nowhere
to go. Can't they ship me back to the States?

– Yes, they can. You'll have to prove you're destitute.

– Prove it! All they have to do is to look inside me. I
ain't even hungry any longer, only indignant.

They both laughed.

He was terribly good-looking, poor kid. She took a fifty-
franc note from her purse and handed it to him.

– What're you doing that for?

But she was walking away now and it was getting him
nowhere, he could feel Angel getting nervous behind his

back, scratching his lighter, nervous bastards those Arabs, not like their camels at all. She was now fifteen yards away, good shooting distance, like in a Gary Cooper movie, pity old Coop was dead now, he'd kind of like him. He liked all sorts of people he had never met.

– Hey!

He walked up toward her. Play it on your looks, close range, you can't miss there.

– I'll pay it back, if you give me half a chance.

– Forget it.

– Well, I mean it. Where can I find you?

Some of those American kids are really terribly good-looking, it's got something to do with the way they're fed when they're babies. She had learned a few things about child care and she had even done some volunteer work in a nursery in Ghana, when they were stationed there.

– You don't have to pay it back. I'm so rich it hurts. Anyway, I'll be around. I'm usually feeding the birds by the bridge over there. Twice a day. You can find me there.

She had a Hebrew lesson with an Israeli student later that day but she could call it off. She was no longer planning to go to work in a kibbutz, anyway. That was last year, after Eichmann's trial. She didn't intend to sit under the bridge waiting for him all the afternoon either. He probably wouldn't turn up anyway, not that it mattered. Pathetic jerk, standing there with his skis, in a strange city and not knowing which way to turn for help. How lost can you get? I better go now, or he'll start imagining things. She waited a moment longer but he was quite hopeless, not a word, and she really had to go now. He waved to her, though, as she drove away, and she waved back, and he stood there grinning.

Silly bitch. He took a cigarette and Angel lit it for him.

– Hooked, Lenny said.

4

A GRAY ASTRAKHAN HAT, A HUGE KHYBER PASS MUS-
tache, a round olive-skinned, pock-marked face—they still
had smallpox out there—a large, bulging Bengal Lancer's
chest, all this was perfectly caught in the Polaroid sights at
the heavenly gates of the Banque Suisse. Now.

– Got him, bwana?
– Right between the eyes.
– Good shot, bwana.

They were long overdue for some big game hunting
in Geneva, Paul said. It's not that I care for the trophy, it's
just that I dislike the animal. Here comes another one.
Egyptian? Tunisian? Moroccan? Nice pelt, anyway.

– Let's get him first, we'll look later.

The Polaroid caught a distinguished-looking, soft-eyed,
voluptuous-lipped little man just as he was pushing the
bank's door.

It took the Polaroid only a few minutes to cook the
game and the two students took a look at the day's trophies.
The soft-eyed Tunisian, the fierce Gunga Din warrior, a
bearded Indian in a turban . . .

– An Indian trader from Durban, who carried his balls in a turban . . . let's skin Gunga Din first . . . look who's going there . . . Jess, hey, Jess!

– I've been looking for you everywhere, kids, Jess said.

– Accomplished any good deeds today, Jessie?

– Yes, I gave myself lunch. What's up?

– Get into the car. And join the Swiss resistance movement. The maquis. The freedom fighters. You see that huge animal leaving the bank? Well, we've just shot him. All we have to do now is to skin the beast and collect the trophy.

– I don't get it, kids. But I'm intrigued. There's nothing more thought-provoking than something you don't understand.

– That's why life is such a kick, Paul said. Get in.

The man with the astrakhan hat was now walking away from the bank and the car crawled slowly behind him.

– What kind of game is this? Jess asked.

– We call it Millions of Dollars. Secret bank accounts, strictly *verboten* by every government in the world but perfectly legitimate in Switzerland . . . Now watch.

The stranger was walking peacefully toward the café.

– He doesn't even realize how badly wounded he is, Paul said. Let's get out.

They followed the astrakhan hat into the café, sat down at a table and ordered three glasses of milk.

– I wonder if we aren't getting a bit too puritanical, Paul said.

– I know, isn't it terrible?

– Particularly you, Jess. You don't even let a fellow sleep with you.

– Yes, I'm a bit antisocial.

– Okay, let's go.

They moved toward the Gunga Din table. Jean was holding the snapshot in his hand.

– Excuse me, sir.

–Please, the man said.

– I wonder if you would be interested in some filthy pictures.

The man's eyes bulged a little and his mustache bristled defensively. Poor little thing, Jess thought. He does look picturesque. Must be a Pathan, they always are. What was that poem again? *There's a boy beyond the river, with a bottom like a peach* . . . Must be Kipling . . . It always is.

– Please, I don't understand, the man said.

– We have here a nice little picture of you entering a Swiss private bank. . . . Now, there is absolutely nothing wrong in having a secret account in a Swiss bank. It's just that it carries the death penalty in your country.

The man seemed to have swollen suddenly. His eyes were bulging. The mustache stood guard valiantly, but you didn't believe in it any more.

– This picture proves nothing.

– That's the spirit. You must never confess. If you confess they will certainly shoot you. If you don't they'll merely confiscate all your property back home. How would you like that picture to appear in the papers back home?

The man was frightened now. He was swallowing hard and there were beads of perspiration on his forehead. Obviously not a Pathan. Pathans are never scared. Or else, perhaps, since they have lost England, they don't care about Kipling any more.

– Are you General Hakim's spies?

– W-w-we are much worse than that, Jean said. Jess simply *adored* the way he stuttered.

– We are S-Swiss p-p-puritans. We are advance elements of the S-Swiss Puritan Army under General C-Calvin's command.

The man was sweating profusely now. It was quite extraordinary to see a Pathan sweat in Geneva.

– I am willing to buy this picture, he said hoarsely.

– Right. We want all the cash you have got and your watch. And your ring. Here's the picture and the negative, with General Calvin's compliments.

– Who is General Calvin?

– He's our spiritual leader. The great mufti of Geneva. He's our local Gandhi, really. You have got twenty-four hours to leave Geneva, after that we'll really give it to you in the Khyber Pass.

She suddenly realized that Paul had been drinking: his face was white and his nostrils were pinched. One day he'll really kill someone, out of sheer love for humanity. They both had a crush on her, but they were good friends, all the same. Last year they went on the Ban-the-Bomb march together, with ten thousand people walking across the peaceful countryside. Kids will always be kids. Some of her friends on that march in England got eighteen months in jail. The judge's name was Sir Archibald Cunningham-Miller. A name for posterity. The poor Pathan didn't know what hit him. No connection whatsoever. The whole relationship between causes and effects is getting out of hand. I think all the kids below twenty-one should be given compulsory anti-rabies shots, so that their parents could feel safe. In the old days they had Hitler, which was nice, you could put it all down to him, but now you had to face the fact that it was practically everybody. If you were a teen-age Puerto Rican or Negro in New York you could always turn juvenile delinquent but if you had a good college education and cultural awareness it was a little more difficult to express yourself fully. The nineteenth-century Russian students used to throw bombs around but it's much more difficult when you believe in Gandhi and nonviolence. They walked out of the café and thoughtfully watched the poor Pathan jump into a taxicab.

– Lovely man, Jess said. I saw pictures in *Time* Magazine showing children starving in his country.

– Careful, Jess, Paul said. You mustn't believe that we have a mission. You mustn't be getting a sacred purpose. That's where the trouble starts. It was just good, clean fun. A students' prank.

– Let's play it again sometime, Jess said. Game therapy. Very good.

The waiter ran out of the café and stared at them with a kind of frightened disbelief.

– Excuse me . . . You have forgotten something. . . .

He was pointing a shaking finger toward the table by the window with the Pathan's roll of banknotes, gold watch and ruby ring lying on it. Paul made a wry face.

– Oh that . . . Throw it away.

The waiter stood there, still pointing to the window, his mouth wide open in an expression of indignant, hurt Swiss surprise.

– W-w-what is the matter? Jean asked. Can't you see it's f-f-filth?

– Might start an epidemic, Jess said. You'd better handle it carefully.

– You can't do that, the waiter said. You can't behave like that. You can't treat money like that. . . .

– Yeah, this is atheism, Jess said.

– Mademoiselle, I could be your father, the waiter said.

– You dirty old man, Jess said, leave my mother alone.

– You can't do this sort of thing in Switzerland, the waiter said.

– Why not? Jess asked. It's only Moral Rearmament. We are conducting a little Moral Rearmament campaign of our own.

They crowded into Paul's car and drove slowly toward the lake.

– It was g-g-good to be able to do s-something about it all, Jean said. Something p-p-positive.

– The Puritan Army is on the march, said Paul. It won't stop short of total victory.

The Quality of Despair, Jess thought. That's a good, Camus-like title. Jess Donahue, winner of the Nobel Prize for literature. Albert Camus, prophet of the absurd, getting killed in an absurd automobile crash, which proves he was wrong and that there is some inner logic in life. Some deeply hidden enjoyment of human drama, but you can't expect a Swiss waiter to understand the irony and the protest. Being young is a desperate business anyway. It always has been. They used to call us the lost generation back in America, forty years ago. Alfred de Musset called it *le mal du siècle,* which was French for *Weltschmerz.* It was there long before the bomb, before the cold war, before atheism. Even in Shakespeare's sonnets you could feel it. It's true that they had syphilis in those days. The sadness of Shakespeare's love sonnets and of all the lyrical poetry in the past was actually due to the fact that love was then so closely associated with syphilis. Everybody had it in those days. You always caught it with love. And it was incurable then, that's why all love poems are so sad and speak of death. Not only did you lose your virginity and become pregnant, but you caught syphilis as well. That's what love meant then. It really meant something to you. There was an interesting paper to be written on the subject. Nobody had brought that up yet. There was no syphilis any more worth speaking of unless you really went out of your way to get it. Perhaps that's why love is no longer

mentioned in modern poetry, it has lost its tragic meaning, the feeling of doom is no longer there, you have to
look for it elsewhere. I wonder what that fellow with the
skis is doing, broke, hungry and not even speaking the
language. I hope I haven't scared him off. I shouldn't
really have told him to meet me where the birds are, he
probably thought I was being facetious. He was so absurdly
good-looking. You could become a nymphomaniac just
trying to help a fellow. Oh well, I suppose I'll never see
him again. Nobody's going to sweep me off my feet, anyway. I wish somebody would, though. Men are all scared
of really bright women. They think they talk in bed. I'll
never talk in bed to any man, no matter what he does. I
suppose in bed you shouldn't even be thinking, just live
and let live.

She still had an hour to kill before fetching her father
and she had the money now, her car tank was full and
they would have *lomble chevalier* for dinner, it was her
father's favorite treat, she had specially ordered it from
Monnier, who was the best *traiteur* in Geneva. It has been
a nice day altogether. Paul's father was a banker and she
had first met Jean when his father was Swiss chargé
d'affaires in Vietnam during the Bao Dai days, and then
later they were in Saudi Arabia together, one of the worst
diplomatic appointments she had ever had, flies, and they
didn't even let you go into a mosque. The diplomatic kids
had a hectic sort of life, being constantly thrown from
one end of the world to the other and always playing

tennis, no matter who was being machine-gunned in the streets, you were always extraterritorial, history was not permitted to touch you, it was only buzzing around your tennis court in a bloody sort of way. You were so well protected that you went to pieces. Diplomatic immunity could do very strange things to you, it was like weightlessness. You had to remind yourself constantly that you actually existed, and you were not supposed to identify yourself too much with the suffering of whatever country you were posted to. But then, who needs reality anyway? And it's no use shouting protests when they know it's only puberty. You have to get over that problem somehow. At one time she had almost decided to let Paul do it, but you couldn't go about a thing like that in a cold-blooded way, there must be something more to it, dammit. After all, people did write some immortal poetry about it. She despised all this "he will do it well" talk, like having the best surgeon to take out your appendix. That was the kind of realistic approach that made French intellectuals such a miserable lot. Whenever a French intellectual talks to you about "freedom" or "revolt," it all somehow boils down to sex in the end. It's probably got something to do with the word *culture* in French, with its etymological root *cul,* which means both ass and sex in the argot. And anyway she and Paul had gone on all the Ban-the-Bomb marches in England, they had set up a local Civil Rights Committee in Geneva and had picketed the Disarmament Commission and so in the end even their personal relationship had also become platonic and it was now very difficult to do something like going to bed together and really facing things. But Paul was still trying, in a very astute, roundabout sort of way:

– I've submitted a terrific plan for action to the Committee of One Hundred, he was saying. What's it all about, I asked them. Obscenity, that's what it's all about. The bomb is pure scientific and moral obscenity. So is the Berlin Wall with the bodies of the killed kids lying on top of it. When Mao Tse-tung tells Nehru he can afford to lose three hundred million people in a nuclear war because there will be still enough Chinese left to savor the fruits of victory over capitalism, it's nothing short of obscenity, nothing but filthy ideological pornography and perversity. Or take the Negro question in the U.S.A.: if that's not obscenity, then what is? When the British judge, Cunningham-Miller, condemns a twenty-year-old Ban-the-Bomb marcher to eighteen months in jail, that's nothing but pornography again. Except that people don't realize it because for them pornography or obscenity has got to have something to do with sex. So you have to give them a clear image of moral debasement, such as they themselves are guilty of, and you have to do it in simple, conventional sexual terms they can understand. All it takes is a deep conviction and a spirit of self-sacrifice, like the Buddhist monks burning themselves alive. That's where we come in, the sons and daughters, preferably those whose parents really mean something in terms of obscenity. The daughter or son of the judge who sent the Ban-the-Bomb marchers to jail should be posing for pornographic pictures and showing them at a press conference to make it clear how he feels about his father's moral standards. It should become a sort of children's crusade, like in the thirteenth century. I submitted a detailed plan to the Nuclear Disarmament Commission but all I got in response was a hurt silence. And yet, if all the kids from here to Peking started copulating in the streets, perhaps our so-called leaders would have a better, clearer image of what they are doing. You don't have to feed us thalidomide to breed monsters. You don't have to throw a bomb to wipe out a whole generation, morally speaking. Overkill is here already. When that pervert Mao Tse-tung says he is willing to sacrifice three hundred million Chinese to see the triumph of socialism, it's breeding monsters all right. But unless we supply them with a good, clear image of what they're about, they'll go on piling on the filth until we have all become such monsters we won't even know we are monstrous. How about it, Jess? Let's stop in front of the Disarmament Commission headquarters, take our clothes off and get down to it. You have to reach them somehow.

– All he is really trying to do is to l-l-lay you, Jess, Jean said. Dialectics.

– Sorry, Paul, but I am simply not idealistic enough, Jess said. I don't live for the bomb alone. I even begin to feel that the only form of social protest worth while is to make a try for some personal happiness.

– How defeatist can you get? Paul muttered.

– No matter how social and progressive you are, you can't escape from the nasty feeling that there is nothing wrong with the world that God couldn't put right in a s-s-second, Jean said. It's a sinking feeling, with all those ch-churches around.

– Immaturity, Paul said.

– It seems that you cannot be an atheist without thinking about G-G-God all the time, Jean said.

– Undergraduate talk, Jess said. God, the bomb, Communist China . . . Some people have real problems, you know.

– Okay, let's have an ice cream, Paul said.

They stopped for a tutti-frutti at the Boissière, then Jess walked to the garage across the street to fetch her car and drove to the clinic.

5

THE PARK WAS BEAUTIFUL, WITH QUIET TREES, YELLOW and white roses everywhere, green pastures with grazing sheep, ponds; it was one of the most expensive institutions in Europe and there was simply no place in the world where a schizophrenic could eat better. The whole idea, apparently, was to interest the patients in reality by all sorts of crafty schemes. The last time she had visited her father she had overheard a conversation between a manic depressive and a paranoiac, who were discussing the comparative merits of a *sole aux bouchées à la Reine* and of a sturgeon *farci à la Vatel*. Some reality. The receptionist, a well-bred, well-groomed, gray-haired woman in a tailored suit, had the bill ready on her desk, but this was one place where they couldn't keep your luggage even though they knew you weren't going to pay. Chic. It was idiotic to worry about financial problems, it was bad enough to be broke. She was determined to see to it that he wouldn't be importuned by the facts of life, at least during the next few days. She had sold his beautiful Russian gold cigarette case but they still had a good Persian rug left and there was always a chance that the State Department would raise their allowance. The only thing that mattered was to present a good façade, you couldn't let your country down, dammit.

– Will you please forward the bill to the Consulate? I don't think my father has his checkbook with him. How is he?

– He has made excellent progress, Miss Donahue. In fact we feel he is completely cured.

Cat's Christmas, Jess thought. I'm twenty-one years old and I have yet to see a chronic alcoholic completely cured. All you can do is to learn how to live with it. One of the most idiotic clichés of psychiatry is that people drink because they can't adjust to reality. The truth of the matter is that any man who can adjust to reality is just a mean son of a bitch.

– You said that the last time, mademoiselle.

Her father was coming down the stairs, a tall, gaunt, handsome man with graying hair, and you could feel the inner strength of the man, the quiet self-confidence, and the dark, humorous eyes that always made you feel like come on, child, tell me your troubles, let me handle that for you. He really deserved some special sort of prize for window dressing. It was just a pity that he was drinking himself to destruction with that smiling, self-assured southern elegance of his and with the dedication that he always put into every good cause he tried to serve. He could have had the richest wives, the most sought-after diplomatic appointments, the most beautiful mistresses; fortunately, he was weak, sensitive, ineffectual and lovable, and so he had only her. He put his arm around her, kissed her on the cheek:

– Let's get the hell out of here, Jessie. I'm dying for a drink.

They laughed and he kept his arm around her shoulders all the way to the car, then he sat quietly while she was taking care of the luggage, and they drove away between the tall old white chestnut trees.

– Well, Jess, tell me the worst. How rapidly are we sinking?

– Nothing to worry about, really. Very much the usual. Honestly, money is like the Communist party. It tells you what you may do, what you may not do, where you may live, where you may not live . . .

– I have devoted my life to the service of my country, it's only natural I should be broke. It's bad enough to fail in what you are trying to do without being well paid for it.

– I sometimes wish you were a son of a bitch, Father. We could have been so happy. And then Mother wouldn't have left you, I suppose.

– Maybe I will still make it someday. I too have my dreams of grandeur.

– How's the problem?

– Under control. I sometimes wake up in the middle of the night, feeling nothing. It's a marvelous sensation. An extraordinary, cool absence of almost everything. You see, I can say I have known happiness. Or sitting in the park on a beautiful night and not thinking or feeling anything. Yes, I have my moments.

– Chekhov, she said.

– I suppose so. What about you, Jess?

– Nothing much. The kids are acting sort of crazy. Everybody is very high on Pope John XXIII, the poor man. There is a fabulous flamenco troupe here, from Seville, Manuelo Vargas, el Guito. I saw them five times. Real gitano stuff. I've written the first sentence of my book: "Living is like beating your wings against a nonexistent windowpane, trying to break through into something that isn't even there. . . ." And I've found a good title for it too: *A Quality of Despair*. It has always been there, I guess, but each generation thinks it's postwar or prewar or cold-war or no-more-war. All I know for sure is that these are pre-something days. Your daughter is getting really exquisite, such delicate yearnings, such soulful nostalgia and subtle *Weltschmerz* moods, I really should carry three Michelin stars for high-quality feelings . . . However, the French are doing fine, and they've been decadent for ages, so I'm not too worried. . . . How is your insomnia?

– I've developed a new technique. Before, I simply lay there for hours until I managed to doze off. Now I'm getting more refined about it. As soon as I fall asleep, I begin to dream that the lights are blazing in the room and that wakes me up immediately.

– How bad was it this time? The "withdrawal process,"
I mean.

– Very much the usual. I met another diplomat there, a
former Swiss Ambassador to Moscow, who spends his days
reading the telephone directory, trying to establish some
sort of contact with reality and real people. He has a very
fine collection of telephone directories from all over the
world, including Moscow. Says it's the greatest book ever
written, full of real people, he has even read some fine
pages of New York aloud to me and sometimes he puts
in a few long-distance calls to check that it's true what the
book says, that it's not just another lie. A very suspicious
sort of fellow but then, after all those years of diplomatic
immunity, I see his point. Sometimes he calls himself on
the phone in the middle of the night, just to make sure
he really exists, that he is not merely lying to himself.
Doesn't trust mirrors a bit, thinks it's some sort of double-
cross. I think I stayed in the diplomatic service too long
and that's part of the trouble. You see too many awful
things happen around you without being part of any of
them and so you end up calling yourself on the phone
every morning just to check if you're real. I am seriously
thinking of resigning from the service, Jess. I've been
looking at some magazines and I think I could find work
as a male model, they seem to like graying, distinguished,
youngish-looking middle-aged men. Schweppes, Camels,
or something like that. Just to prove to the whole world
that Alan Donahue still has it in him. You'll probably
think I'm being overconfident . . .

– I wish you'd stop trying to get rid of yourself, Father dear. That's all your sense of humor is really about.

– In the meantime I've made up my mind about a rather important matter. You see, I haven't wasted my time in the clinic. Yes, I have been thinking. I feel I've been a little slack in the performance of my duties. Not serving the high aims of our foreign policy to the best of my capacity. We are going to give a party, Jess. Yes, I mean it. . . . If my memory is good, our last cocktail party goes back to the days when the Berlin Wall went up. Nothing extravagant, a hundred people or so. We can sell my gold cigarette case. That ought to put us back on the map.

– Seriously, what *are* we going to do about Berlin?

– We aren't going to ask the Russians to the party, that's what we're going to do about it.

– Don't clown, please. They've covered the whole Students' Club with blown-up pictures of the boy they left to die on the Berlin Wall. . . .

– Kids will always be kids.

– And then you are supposed to go to class and study literature. . . .

– I promised the doctors not to touch the stuff any more. One glass of wine with my meals, that's all. That's the only statement I can make at this moment.

He had taken a slip of paper from the glove compartment.

– "Samson Delila and his Pussycats" . . . What on earth can that be? Darling Jess, why are you crying?

– I sold your gold cigarette case a week ago. The grocer

was getting really mad. We still have the Persian carpet, though. . . . Oh, it's some French rock-'n'-roll group, like the *"Chausettes noires,"* you know. . . . It's such a mess, such a mess. It can't go on much longer. I'm beginning to lose interest in survival.

– Samson Delila and his Pussycats, really . . . What next? Maybe they've got a point, though. They seem to be accepting gallantly the challenge of universal insanity. I think we ought to go and listen to them. They seem to have something to say.

– They're no good. Ray Charles is coming back next week and I may be able to get some tickets. You really ought to try him. The Negroes are the only people in the world who seem to have an answer. I suppose James Baldwin would hate me for saying so.

– You know, their smiles seem bigger only because they have got more lip, Jess.

– I guess they're quite right in trying to get away from that fun label, but I wish they wouldn't. If you take my illusions about the Negro race away from me, the hope that they are just a little different, then I don't know, I really don't know. I fully understand, of course, that they don't want to be loved any more, they are only human, after all. But equal rights: *tu te rends compte?* Equal rights with whom? With what? I cannot imagine Ray Charles accepting equal rights, with the sort of rights there are around. The worst indignity we have done the Negroes is that we made them so keen to share what we've got, what we are doing and what we are. How low can you sink? Oh, Father, stop making fun of me. Your eyes are laughing again. You never take me seriously. I know I'm a joke, but I'm *your* joke, remember that. You made that one. And it's pretty bad style to laugh at your own jokes.

– All I mean is that we should be happy to have some personal problems, Jess. It takes the mind off other things. To worry yourself sick for strictly personal reasons gives one a wonderful feeling of luxury. Such a pleasant change. In a truly successful society you can be unhappy only for personal reasons. Everything else has been solved. That's why America and Soviet Russia are such happy countries.

– You're very good company, Father, I know that. But what *are* we going to do?

– There's one thing that baffles me in our financial situation, Jess. We live across the border in France. Twenty minutes' drive and we are in Geneva. That was your idea, a stroke of genius. It gives us two countries where we can pile up debts instead of the usual one. An ideal position for a minor diplomat. How come, then, we have hit bottom so quickly here, too?

– It's the combination of the Swiss and the French together. It's about the worst you can get. They are totally untrustworthy. Cynical. They've seen it all. You can go shopping dressed by Balenciaga, but they'll know you're broke. They are the most sensitive and perceptive people in the world when it's money. A very old civilization, I suppose.

– Oh, hell, Samson Delila and his Pussycats to it all. You will manage somehow, Jess. You always do. I trust you completely about these practical things.

The cherry and apple trees were in full bloom all the way from Geneva to the French frontier and this was the season of the yellow and white butterflies, thousands of them floating around, and she hated to see them crashing into the windshield and dying, their broken little bodies glued to the glass, but she was not going to let herself be upset by it, you've got to stop somewhere. It was their problem. She was hardening up, developing a strong self-protecting instinct at long last. Even so she experienced her usual rather guilty, Rolls-Royce feeling as the Swiss and French frontier guards waved aside the other cars to let them pass across the frontier, with a *"Bonjour, Mademoiselle Donahue, mes respectes, Monsieur le Consul,"* while the other drivers looked at them and their CC plates with a typically French democratic hatred for their kin. It was a good life if you could only get rid of that absurd feeling of financial insecurity.

The house was a hundred yards away from the road and she could still smell the lilacs and the roses as she opened the door and went in, carrying the food basket, everything was going to be all right somehow, but then, as she went back from the kitchen to the living room, she took one look at his shoulders—he was standing with his back to her, reading his mail in the yellow twilight by the window—and she heard the sharp tone of anger in her own voice, she always got angry when she was scared:

– What is it this time, for God's sake? What is it?

He turned his head toward her slowly. But then you could not get anything from his face. It was the only thing in life that he had under perfect control. The irony was always there, spread all over once and for all, and it was one of those faces with strong features that could hide almost anything. Maybe it's only a letter from America saying that her mother died. Or maybe they were posted to Nigeria, Lagos, the worst climate in the world. Well, she would collect African masks and sculptures. She was trying desperately to strike a bargain with fate.

– Bad news?

– Sorry, Jess, I'm fired. Retired, that is. Same thing.

– Now of all the rotten, low tricks . . . I had dinner with Granville only two days ago, he didn't say anything.

– Tact.

– Yes, I know. Tactful bastards.

– Let's be fair, Jess. My usefulness to the service was no longer strikingly evident.

– Are you going to defend State again?

– Why should the American taxpayer support a chronic alcoholic?

– Because he is the American taxpayer. Isn't that a good enough reason? He has supported almost everything else, hasn't he?

He did laugh, thank God. That was the only strength left in him, his sense of humor. She was sitting in a chair with the food basket on the floor between her legs, wondering where the next joke would come from. No matter how funny it would be, she was not going to cry. They were smiling at each other quite convincingly. Style.

– Isn't it wonderful, Jess? You are no longer responsible for American foreign policy. The world can go to hell now, it's no longer our problem.

– Yes, let's celebrate.

She went to the kitchen and opened a bottle of cider. It had some alcoholic content, but what the hell. There was a note from the maid on the table: *"Mademoiselle, je veut etre payer ou je vai au tribunal."* Three bad spelling mistakes in one sentence. She made a lot of noise with the bottle and glasses, went back into the living room with the tray and there he was, his dark, humorous eyes showing the light of an unbroken spirit.

– Let's drink to independence, Father dear.

– Cheers!

– Do you know what Napoleon said coming back home after the Moscow retreat, disaster, millions of dead, and finding his wife in bed with some guy?

– What?

– He said: *"Eh bien,* It's nice to have some good personal problems for a change." It's in Louis Bertrand's book.

– We must all study the life of Napoleon so as to avoid making the same mistakes. Cheers!

– Cheers!

Oh well, she thought, strong, hard and ruthlessly purposeful men are everywhere. They are the ones who make the world such a smashing success. But it's the weak, vulnerable and ineffectual men like you who undo all their good work and make the world still human and lovable. I don't think I could love you more even if you were both Jewish and a Negro.

She put the glasses back on the tray.

– I've got to go back to Geneva, do you mind? Shan't be long. Do you know a count from Altenberg? Hangs around. He's offered me a job. I turned him down at first, but I hear he's a big-time crook, so maybe it's something serious.

– Jess . . .

– Oh, all right. I'm going to see Mr. Granville and ask him a few questions. They don't fire people from the State Department simply because they are alcoholics. Becoming one is part of the job and part of our foreign policy. It's an idealistic policy, after all, so what do they expect?

– There's absolutely nothing he can do about it.

– I know. But I need to let off steam and he's got a heart condition, hasn't he? It's pure, healthy aggressiveness, that's all.

– Yes, it's only normal you should be aggressive, Jess dear. You're my daughter.

Yes, I know, but apparently you can laugh at yourself all your life and still need a bottle of whiskey a day to finish the job. She had a good cry in the car, driving slowly, trying to prepare some sarcastic, scathing, mockingly wounding things she was going to say to the Consul-General, and make him feel simply awful, she'd be ironic and biting, so scornful in a detached, sophisticated way. But then, as she stopped her car in front of the building, she just sat there, what's the use, he is only going to play Menotti's *Consul* for me: There is absolutely nothing I can do, my dear, the decision has been taken in Washington, the State Department did not even consult me, which I find rather high-handed.

Surely they can't dismiss a man from the service just like that. . . .

Your father has not been dismissed, my dear. He has been retired, which is not the same thing. Not the same thing at all.

But he had at least eight years more to go.

You know the reason as well as I do.

All right, so he drinks. Who doesn't?

During the past four years Alan had to spend six months in different clinics. It didn't seem to help. The State Department had to move him from one country to another. These things get around quickly and for an American representative abroad . . . You know how it is. . . .

Yes, I know how it is. But I still have moments of disbelief. Montaigne said that a strong capacity for disbelief is essential to survival. The moment you begin to believe your eyes, you catch reality and then why bother to live at all?

This last bit is not Montaigne at all, it's Jessica Donahue, *A Quality of Despair*. Sitting in her little Sunbeam in a street in Geneva, speaking her mind to the American Consul-General, letting him have it right between the eyes. It was about time somebody did that. She'd walk into the office and shoot him dead with a few well-chosen words.

Do you know why my father has become a hopeless alcoholic, sir? I can tell you that. La Paz, Bolivia. The highest capital in the world. Fourteen thousand feet. Four years. You can hardly breathe, but it helps to drink a little. Then Bulgaria, three years behind the Iron Curtain, during the worst period of the cold war. You make some friends and they get ten years in jail simply because they've had dinner with you. You tell Stavrov that the U.S. Government will never let the democratic process down and six weeks later Stavrov is hanged. So you drink a little more than you used to. You ask to be recalled in protest and this is interpreted as a sign that you overidentify with the interests of the country you are accredited to. This makes you eligible for transfer to Habad on the Persian Gulf, which is no country at all, so you can't identify with anything except sand and flies. A hundred and fifteen degrees of heat all year round, and so you drink a little more than you used to. Then Moscow, where all the diplomats are considered spies unless they agree to spy for the Russians, which is *kharasho*. Your wife cannot take it. She tells you to resign or else. But by now you are in your late forties and you have a daughter and you don't have the guts to resign from the service and to look for a job, so your wife leaves you, she's tired of changing lovers all the time, she wants security. So you drink a little more than you used to. Then suddenly Greece, ten cocktail parties a week, a whirl of gay, pleasant people, but you have to entertain, so you make debts. And you worry. And the more you worry, the more you drink. And so on and so on, until suddenly you discover that you can't stop drinking and that you can't pay your debts and these things get around quickly, and so quite naturally your government decides it has no more use for you.

Yes, I know. I know only too well, my dear. But I have to add something. Painful as it may be for you, I'm going to put it quite bluntly, because we all know you here as a strong, very intelligent girl. We don't all take to drink and make debts. It is a matter of . . . character.

I think I had better go.

I am sorry. Alan is a nice, honorable man, brilliant in many ways, but he has chosen the wrong profession. He is too sensitive. A career diplomat cannot afford sensitivity. He needs hard eyes. Our job is to observe history in the making, with sympathy and compassion of course, but from outside. We are observers.

Voyeurs.

You may put it that way.

Goodbye, sir.

Goodbye, Jess. I hope both of you will come and have dinner with us next week. My wife likes you a lot.

Thank you.

Please let me know if there is anything at all I can do.

The son of a bitch. There was absolutely no point in talking to him. She started her car and drove slowly toward the bridge across from the Hôtel des Bergues, feeling so helpless that the only positive thing she could think of was to go down to the landing on the lake and feed the seagulls and the ducks. She worked twice a week at the SPCA and it helped her a lot, but this was not her day. The vet there was a nice, gruff man and she missed him often. She threw some bread to the ducks and Lord Byron rushed like mad toward her and settled in her lap. Only a Pavlov reflex, of course. But it's no good looking at things too closely. He only loves you because you feed him. Everything boils down to economics. Very few people who have pets actually kill themselves. If Marilyn Monroe had had someone to look after, or if she had worked at the SPCA, or knew a nice vet, she would probably be still alive today. She kissed him on the beak and his marmalade-colored neck, and sat there, back against the wall, holding him. You'll have to face it someday, kid. Love, the lack of it.

– Hi!

She didn't really expect him until tomorrow morning, somehow. She was not really looking for him here, it was only a vague hope. She hid her face in the duck's wet feathers and smiled a little. Hi, really. Why not "howdy, partner?" Kid stuff. Brought up on television serials, I suppose.

– Hello.

– How come there are seagulls in Switzerland?

She didn't even dare to look up at him. Unsure of herself. Good girl. I bet my last pair of pants she is a virgin. It's so ready to snap she's scared to look at you. Thinks it shows in her eyes. It does, too. The way she's been clinging to that duck for the last fifteen minutes, you'd think she's got nowhere to go. He put his skis against the wall, sat down on his heels close to her.

– So far inland, I mean? And the mountains. They can't fly that high. Not the seagulls, anyway.

– All kinds of strange birds come to Switzerland.

– Thanks. Lenny's the name, by the way. Seriously, I don't get it. The sea's an awful long way off. Wonder what brings them here?

– Security. That's what Switzerland is famous for. They have security here. They know they'll be fed.

Sharp. You've got to be careful with her. That's why she's still a virgin, probably. Scares them off. Try that on me, baby. May take me more than three days, though. The way to do it is to play it so lost and dumb she'll get to feel about me the way she feels about that duck. Protective. Pity it's got to be me. She deserves a better deal. Well, that's the way the cookie crumbles. Maybe I'll teach her skiing some day so that it won't all be a dead loss for her. Anyway, there's no point in disliking yourself simply because you happen to be human. What else can you expect from sperm?

– They know they'll be fed. The whole of Switzerland

is one big bird sanctuary. They come here from all over the world. Emigrés.

– What?

– Refugees. Bulgars, Czechoslovaks. All sorts. The Swiss don't touch them, they only watch them carefully. They're a nation of bird watchers. Why do you carry your skis with you all day long?

– A fellow's got to stick to something. Hell, I wish I were a seagull. I hear they can sleep on the water just drifting along. That's living.

– Is it that bad?

– I didn't say that. But it sure ain't easy, trying not to sink to the bottom, I mean, like taking a job and all that.

She laughed.

– A ski bum in summer, eh?

– Right. I'm bumming around, trying to see as much snow as I can. That's all I'm good at, skiing. It's okay in winter, when they need instructors everywhere, you can make a living and have your fun, but summertime it gets tough. Real tough. I suppose I'll survive until the snow, but don't ask me how.

– Can't you get a job for the summer?

– I don't give up that easy.

– You're a funny one.

Yeah. The way you look at me, kid, you must be starving for a joke.

– Why don't you go back home?

– What d'you mean, home? What's that?

She's sweet when she's laughing, she sure is.

– It's a household word.

– Let's keep vocabulary out of it. Never helped anyone.

– What do the skis stand for? Freedom? Escape? Getting away from things?

That's how she scares them away. Brains. Poor kid. No wonder she's still new.

– They're just skis.

– Can't you leave them somewhere when you're in town? They must be heavy.

– You don't get arrested as a vagrant when you carry a pair of skis. You can sleep under a bridge or on a bench, the cops take a look at the skis and they know you're all right. Don't ask me why, but it's a fact. Maybe because they smell clean. The skis, I mean. Snow.

– You've been around, haven't you?

– I've learned a few things. Experience. You can get too much of it, though. Got to know where to stop.

She looked at him critically. Poor bastard, but she was not going to get involved. She wasn't going to be swept off her feet by a good-looking guy with nowhere to go.

They were both looking fixedly at Lord Byron but never did a duck get less attention.

– Have you been to the consulate?

– No. It scares me, kind of.

– Why? It's their job to look after American citizens in trouble.

– I don't think of myself as a citizen. I still have some

self-respect left. They got me real scared back home with that citizen crap. I was walking the street one day and then I see a poster with a finger pointed at me, saying: "Don't ask what your country can do for you, ask what you can do for your country." That did it. I got out real fast.

That's okay, even if it's true, in a way, you can give her that, it's good antisocial stuff, she'll dig it, she almost smiled. Conformity. You've got to be conventional with a kid like that, you've got to make some sense to her.

– I can't go to the consulate, they've got papers on me. I'm a draft dodger. They want my passport back. They always try to get you back one way or the other. The other day I went down the Kirchen Range and there was a guide with a stop watch in his hand looking at me. Eh, he says, do I know you? I just shake my head. Well, he says, I ought to. You made that run in sixteen seconds, which is almost as good as the Olympic record. I didn't mean to, I told him. I didn't like the way that guy looked at me, noticing me, you know what I mean. You're American? Yeah, I told him. Well, you ought to try for the American Olympic team, he tells me. He gave me his card, too. Mike Jones, you know, the former champion, training the American team for the Olympics out here. I told him I wanted to make no team, American or otherwise. They always try to get you back, the bastards. They don't even respect Swiss neutrality. Maybe I'll try Outer Mongolia someday. They've got the best nothing there.

He had her laughing, which was fine. Sympathy. You had to have that. The kid had a big heart, just as she had big everything. How she'd managed to stay a virgin with a heart like that was some question. Luck, probably. She had to be lucky.

– So what are you going to do?

– Something will come up. I got arrested once in Zermatt and the cop's family fed me for weeks afterward. They don't often have a chance to feed an American in Europe. Makes them feel big. Superior, kind of. Makes them feel they really have it good, and then I've got an engaging personality. I get sympathy. Good cowboy type. They think they've seen me in the movies. I'll get by.

Now don't get too clever, Lenny boy. Won't do. Won't do at all. You'll only begin to look smart-ass and that's not the way to make a girl feel maternal and protective about you. That's not the way to make a girl, period.

– What're you doing in Geneva? Aside from being alive, I mean.

– I'm studying at the University.

– Studying what?

– Social science and literature. I take history too.

I shouldn't have told him that. He'll probably think I talk in bed. Not that I care. To hell with him. I can't sit here the whole day holding this duck.

– Social science, eh?

– Don't jump to conclusions. I didn't write those posters for Kennedy. I've got to go now. Good luck.

– Don't forget to feed the ducks tomorrow.

Sweet. And so terribly good-looking. Lovely blond hair. She didn't like blond men at all, as a rule.

– I won't.

Now he was fussing with his skis again and it was so clear that he didn't know what to do and where to go that she couldn't help smiling. She simply had to do something to help and anyway she was sick and tired of thinking about herself all the time. When you have more personal problems than you can cope with, try to help someone. Good therapy. Maybe it sounds a little selfish but then you could do with a little selfishness for a change. There must be a lot of people who give themselves away to humanity simply to escape their personal mess. Was it La Rochefoucauld or Chamfort who said that selflessness is running away from yourself? It must have been La Rochefoucauld. It always is. She threw the last crumbs of bread to the birds.

– Why don't you come home with me? We could put you up for a while. My father won't mind.

It shook him, sort of. It made him feel quite a bit angry and sad, all of a sudden. He thought there was more to her than that. Maybe she doesn't mean it, though. Maybe she's got purity. Anyway, there's no use feeling such a louse because you happen to be one. It's summer and you've got to do the same as anyone else. You've got to live. And loving is part of living, no question about that.

– What sort of father is he? They make me nervous.

– I've made the offer.

– I'll take you up on that one. Only for one night or two, mind you. I never stick. Thieves' honor.

– One night or two is all we're good for, anyway. We have to pay the rent Wednesday, and we're broke.

– How come? I thought you were official.

– Let's not get into that.

Now I'd better let Angel know it's in the bag and we're in. I've got to fetch that suitcase somehow. It'll be all over by tomorrow. Nobody hurt. Maybe she'll wonder a bit for a day or two. But she'll get over it fast enough. You can get around the world in twenty-four hours nowadays, all of India, Brazil, Africa, sure she knows that. Modern.

– Give me five minutes. I mean I've got to grab my bag and a shirt. . . . Now if I come back here and find you gone, it's okay. I won't mind. It was nice talking to you anyway.

What a pathetic jerk. Anxious, almost scared. They must have hurt him a lot. It's quite encouraging to find somebody even more confused and frightened than yourself. It's wonderful to see how much human beings can do for each other.

– I'll be waiting in the car.

His face brightened up considerably and made him look younger than he probably was. Just a kid, really. I'm quite safe there. You didn't have to be very perceptive to feel that. And you didn't need to be very perceptive either to guess that he had never had much of a mother. Nobody has, it seems.

– You know, this is the best thing that's happened to me in a lifetime.

Must have been some lifetime, she thought. But then lifetimes always are.

It was five minutes' walk to the harbor from the bridge. The yacht was wide and big and it seemed a waste to use it on a lake, it could cross the Atlantic easily. Finding yourself on a yacht in mid-ocean must really be something worth living for. You can't stay there forever but at least you know where you belong. Once you are out there in mid-ocean, all you need is no company, no engine and no sails, almost no boat. That would be home. Complete security.

He crossed the deck and went down to the cabin. The door was open. Angel was lying on the berth, all dressed with his hat on. A Negro girl sat at his feet, all dressed too. It was kind of funny that he should've caught them dressed. Angel was a first-class son of a bitch. He didn't want to get too involved or too intimate to make it personal so he never bothered to undress. An Arab, a Negro, an American. That's Geneva. The girl was holding a dead seagull in her lap.

– It crashed on the deck, the girl said.

– Next time, you knock, Angel told him.

– We're in, Angel. I'm spending the night at their house. Tell the boss. Who is he, anyway?

– Who's the boss here, Lenny? Some question you're asking. No boss. Me and you.

– She's an early riser. Feeds the birds at dawn. That sort of kid.

– I'll be there.

– Crashed on the deck at my feet, just like that, the girl said.

– I knew you didn't do it, Lenny said. Relax.

– Next time, you knock, Angel said. I'm not always making love here. Might be something important.

The Negro girl was crying now.

– Come on, it was only a gull, Lenny said.

– It's not only that, the girl said. It's . . . everything.

– That makes it easier, Lenny said. If it's everything, forget it.

– I don't even know why I came to Europe, the girl said. It's funny. Back home, I thought it was because I was colored. But here I really don't know why anything any more. I prefer the way you feel in the United States. At least there's a reason for it, you're colored. You know you've got a problem. But here it's much worse. You can't even blame it on the problem. They haven't got one here. It's general. It sort of takes your illusions away.

– You should've taken your clothes off, Lenny said. You'd have felt less bad. More important. Anyway, I hear they're pushing new legislation through Congress.

– Perhaps I ought to go back home, the girl said. At least, I know what it's all about back there.

– It's under the bed, Angel said.

Lenny took the valise.

– Here it's got nothing to do with being colored, the girl said. They make you feel the same like anyone else.

– You go back home, kid, Lenny said.

– It's got nothing to do with being colored here, the girl said. You don't know anything any more.

Dope, Lenny thought.

– And then the seagull, the girl said. It just crashed at my feet like that, there.

– I'll be seeing you, Lenny said.

He went up on the deck. The stupid bitch, he thought. She made sense, though. Color had nothing to do with it.

6

SHE TURNED ON THE RADIO AS SOON AS THEY WERE IN
the car, there was nothing they could possibly have to say to
each other, anyway. She struck it rich: Martial Solal at the
piano, the best thing that happened to France since Django
Reinhardt. A parody of the best there is in jazz, from The-
lonius Monk to Art Tatum, with a pastiche of almost everything there has ever been in jazz thrown in, which was
exactly what Nabokov was doing in *The Gift* and *Pale Fire*,
a parody—the pastiche of great Russian literature done
with a kind of self-mocking desperation that always ends in
something the Germans call *Lustmörd*. Nabokov gives you
the feeling that no matter how passionately you make love
to literature, she always says "no" to you even during the
act. That ought to keep him in his place, she thought. She
knew exactly how to handle him. She did catch him peep-
ing at her breasts and her thighs once or twice. Oh well,
I do look rather misleading. Not intellectual at all, which
is perhaps just as well, it would only scare him. She managed to catch sight of him in the mirror from time to time
and once their eyes met in the mirror and he grinned,

which was a little annoying. One of those blond god types she didn't go for at all, with dark green eyes, but he probably didn't know how good-looking he was. There couldn't be much going on in that pretty head. Dumb. Inarticulate. One couldn't help feeling sorry for the poor bastard, so lost. He seemed a little surprised when the frontier guards on both the French and the Swiss sides waved them through without asking them for their papers.

– Do they always let you pass like that?

– Diplomatic immunity. That's what the CC plates are for, *Corps Consulaire*. They have no right to open my bags or look into the luggage compartment or anything. International courtesy.

– Is that so? Well, what d'you know?

I suppose he's never heard about diplomatic immunity in all his life. I hope it doesn't scare him off completely. A real bum, doesn't know anything about anything. Never knows what will hit him next. Then one day he'll find himself married to some ugly powerhouse with glasses, who's managed to get herself pregnant, the fool. He sits there, struck dumb, doesn't dare open his mouth, knows he'll only say something stupid. Quite disappointing, in a way. Some adventure. Maybe he's a fag, dammit. It reaches the point where they just sit with their knees tightly pressed together and wait for the girl to take the first step. The hell I will. I'm not running for matriarchy. Well, that's too bad. You've got a problem, kid.

She caught his eyes in the mirror again and smiled reassuringly. I'm going to eat you. I suppose he feels I'm too sophisticated for him. What does he expect me to do, take his hand? Not while I'm driving. He's very sweet, though. Perhaps I ought to say something to make him less tense.

– Do you like jazz?

He grinned.

– Listen, kid, you don't have to communicate. It's okay. I know it shows.

– It shows? What on earth do you mean?

– I left school when I was fourteen. You had a lot of education, I can see that. And you've got class. It's written all over you. So I better tell you right away. I'm a bum, all of me.

Class, really.

– I despise that word.

– Okay, I take it back.

– What did you say your name was?

That's a pathetic trick, he thought. Class my ass. She's slipping.

– Lenny. I don't know what I'm talking about, anyway. I hate vocabulary. It's all propaganda. You know something? I've never seen a girl like you. And beginning tomorrow I'll probably never see one again.

She laughed.

– You don't have to run away.

She's coming along fine, just fine.

– You got me almost worried.

– Now, come on.

– You're bad for my principles.

– What are your principles, exactly?

– That it's all . . . I don't want to be rude. I've always felt pretty sure there's nothing worth while except skiing. You make me wonder now. I suppose nothing of this makes sense to you?

– It does too.

He shook his head.

– Well, it doesn't to me. It's all vocabulary. Words. They're full of vocabulary, back home. Big country, big words. I guess they're full of it in Europe too, only I don't speak the language, so I'm okay. It's all apple orchards around here. Pretty, kind of.

– What are you going to do?

– I don't know. I don't make plans for myself just because I happen to be alive. The white are the cherry trees, eh? I don't like thinking about myself, anyway. I don't see the point.

– You've got to live.

– Who said that?

– You sure seem to be as far away from home as you can get.

– I guess so.

She was so disturbed she almost missed the turning. She caught it just in time and drove through the orchard toward the house.

– Hey, this is beautiful. There must be thousands of trees here. . . .

It was quite touching to see how delighted he looked. Pathetic jerk.

There was a note from her father telling her he wouldn't be back for dinner. She was a little embarrassed to find herself alone with him in the house, not that it mattered, but it made her feel a little self-conscious. The *lomble chevalier* was still on the tray in the kitchen and she decided she might as well feed him. No use wasting a good dish. She found him standing in the hall looking at the portrait on the wall.

– Who is this?

– Nicolas Stavrov. A Bulgarian. He was hanged in 1948. He was a friend of my father's.

– What did they hang him for?

– Politics.

– Some world. I'm glad I'm out of it.

– Don't you have a family?

– I made a girl pregnant once. I don't know what happened to it. Her fault, anyway.

– What do you mean, her fault?

– She wanted a child. She didn't tell me that, she just grabbed it. Some trick.

– What happened to her?

– I don't know. I haven't been looking.

Well, at least that's loud and clear, she thought.

– I'll make us some coffee.

I don't know why I'm giving her all this crap. The fish tasted good. I know, though. I'm trying to warn her, that's what it is. I'm giving her a good chance. I like her. The best fish I ever had. She sure would make a wonderful wife for somebody else. She's full of lovely kiddies, four, five of them. Sweet little faces. He had to laugh.

– What is it, Lenny?

– Best fish I ever had.

– I still can't see the joke.

She felt a little hurt. He was sitting there laughing his head off. And they were alone in the house. Really.

– Sorry. I don't mean to be rude. I just couldn't help that. Maybe it's the food. My first square meal in weeks. I always get high when I suddenly eat on an empty stomach.

– Would you like some more coffee?

– No thanks. I've got to be careful. I don't want to remember it too much.

– It's only coffee.

– Yeah, I suppose so.

He had a fantastic smile, gay, you wanted to see it again and again. You felt like doing something to make him smile again. I've felt suicidal all day and this is what's known as a golden opportunity. He could do that for me. I feel like getting rid of myself once and for all and at least it would be somebody nice and worth while. It would be unfair to him, though. It would hit him too hard and he's down already. Down and out . . . You have to think, unfortunately. Sex is really getting rid of oneself, a ten-minute suicide. Ten minutes or whatever it is, I have no idea. But I'm not going to do it, of course. I don't want to hurt him. I can't give him so much suddenly and then send him back next day where he came from, nowhere. He'll only hate the world even more and he'll probably even begin to take his skis to bed with him. It's up to him, anyway. And I'd better stop looking at him or he'll think I have a crush on him. He's confused enough as it is.

– Why did they hang that Bulgarian, did you say?

– Progress.

– I'll help you do the washing-up.

I should get up and turn the light on. It's quite dark in here.

– It can wait. I'll show you your room.

She picked up his valise. Light. I bet he hasn't even got a shirt in here. I have to show him the room now. It's all right, he won't dare. I just hate walking upstairs in front of a guy. I must try to lose weight. He can probably hear my heart beating, it's so loud. All hearts are idiots. If he tries something I'll never see him again. I'm looking so damned severe and composed, he'll never dare. I'll make it really hard for him. I'll just say no. Nicely, but firmly, without hurting his feelings or anything. God, I do hate myself. I'm a sex maniac, that's what I am. He probably doesn't even think about it. Too humble. Knows his place. God, I don't know how to handle it at all.

She opened the door.

– Goodnight. Breakfast at six.

– What's the matter? What've I done wrong?

– What on earth are you talking about?

– You look mad at me.

– I had a rough day.

I'm a stupid cow and a coward, that's what I am and I wish I were dead.

No, kid, I'm not going to do it. I like you. I have a job to do but that's not what I'm paid for. I sure don't like to hurt a girl that's all new. If you really mean it, fine, I'll give it to you, but you have to ask for it. Maybe it would do you a lot of good but it's for you to say. Don't stand there, trembling. I want you to have a good time if I'm to get on with it and you're too damned panicky now. You want it so badly you're rigid with fear. Paralyzed. You'll only make me mess up the job. You go to bed like a good girl. If you really mean it, okay, you have all night to make up your mind. Jesus, she's got tears in her eyes now. Wait a minute, I know how to handle this. I'll make a big, clumsy pass at you and you'll send me packing and that'll make you feel better. Pride. I'm going to help you as best I can. Here, let me make that lousy pass at you so you won't feel rejected. It'll clear the air.

She pushed his arm away.

– No, she said. Please don't.

– Why not?

– And then what?

– What d'you mean, then? There's no such thing. Then I'll go away. Nobody hurt. It won't last so there'll be nothing to worry about.

– Sorry. Doesn't sound like me, Lenny.

– Why're you crying?

– Why? Why everything? I don't know. Please let go.

– Okay. I could marry you sure enough but I like you too much for that. I wouldn't do that to you.

She was smiling now. She still held her hanky to her eyes but she was smiling. She was no longer scared or stiff. It worked.

He's such a nice boy, she thought. She felt so confident and relaxed now she could almost do it. If he would only put his arms around my shoulders and try to kiss me again, I'd let him do it. But he won't. He's too gentle and considerate. I've probably scared him away forever.

– You're nice, Lenny. Please forgive me.

Now she's all soft and ready.

– Well, goodnight, Jess.

– Goodnight.

– I didn't mean to offend you or anything. . . .

– I know that.

She's asking for it now. She's all opened up. She's lucky it's me.

– I wish I could . . . I wish I were different. . . .

Sure, sure. For crying out loud. Maybe I should. Lenny the good Samaritan. What's that word? Conscience. Vocabulary again. I've still got some vocabulary shit left. So far from home, and still there. Doesn't rub off easy, I guess. Sticks.

– Why're you laughing? I know I'm foolish.

– It's not that, Jess. I wasn't thinking about you.

– Well, thanks.

– I was thinking about myself. Don't be sore at me. Anyone can tell I'm a jerk.

– Don't say that. It's my fault.

– Well, goodnight.

– Goodnight, Lenny. Please try to understand.

– Yeah, yeah. I've been doing just that for the last twenty years. Goodnight.

– Goodnight.

I bet she's still standing behind that door. He went to the window, began to undress, looking at the sky. Nothing there. Conscience. Vocabulary. That stuff sure clings. You must still have some good old American earth clinging to your heels, you bastard. But I've got to do a dirty job on her and two dirty jobs in one night on the same kid would be too much of a good thing. You got to know your limits. I'm only a ski bum in summer. I'm not trying to break any shit records, only to make a little dough to tide me over. I wish I were back up there in the snow. Closer to nothing. Maybe you've got to die first. I shouldn't have let her take the suitcase, she could feel it was empty. Aw, who cares.

There was a Swiss cuckoo clock over the bed. He climbed under the blanket. There's no place like home.

7

SHE WAS A BIT UPSET AND ANGRY WITH HERSELF AND for no reason at all: after all, she did handle it quite well. She was sure she didn't hurt him. It was always difficult to show friendliness and even liking while turning a fellow down, but she felt she had managed to do precisely that with a considerable amount of *savoir-faire*. I only hope he doesn't feel rejected and hurt and miserable. I would, probably. Perhaps I ought to go and talk to him and explain it a little better: you cannot go to bed with a guy just because you're utterly unhappy and wretched and wish to get rid of yourself and he happens to be around. Then, of course, you'll never see him again and he'll keep wondering what hit him. It would be unfair to him. It might even give him some sort of traumatic shock. And yet he wanted it so badly, so humbly too, didn't dare to insist. I'm such a selfish bitch, truly. I hope he doesn't think I'm frigid. Maybe I am. God, that would be terrible. Some women never come around until quite late. Wolfe wrote that eighty-five percent of American females are partly frigid, and at least twenty-five percent totally. I wonder what he means by partly frigid: you've got to stop somewhere. Sex is such utter nonsense, it's an insult to human dignity. They really should have invented another way for making love than *that*. All this sticking-in business is positively revolting. I wonder how Pope John is doing. The news flash said he was quite sick. He's the most lovely man of the century and I adore him. He has such big, sweet ears, rather like an elephant. And so human, not at all a puritan. He would understand. It's beginning to rain. I used to love the sound of the rain on the roof, but tonight it feels lonely. It must be the most beautiful sound in the world when you're with someone you really love, not just sex. Seems to be Father's night out. He'll probably come home with a relapse, begging to be forgiven. I've got enough money to pay the rent, but what about the rest? I wonder if he's asleep already? I bet he can't sleep. I know exactly how he feels and it's my fault. I felt like going through with it. I still do, let's face it. Or at least lying in his arms, listening to the rain on the roof. That's all. We don't have to go further than that. It must be such a beautiful sound, after you've gone through with it and got rid of yourself and of all your problems. I've absolutely no guts. Oh God, I'm a mess. I think of nothing but myself all the time.

The sound of the rain was gentle and soothing and he would be asleep by now. Oh well. She leaned out of bed, switched on the transistor. They had killed another civil rights leader in Mississippi, and it was officially admitted now that radioactivity in fallout areas was twice as high this year as the accepted maximum. But somehow it didn't help this time. It didn't work. She couldn't concentrate on something really important. She couldn't get rid of herself and her whole body was aching with longing, a selfish, physical longing. There was a dead hush and then the news bulletin began again and as she groped for the switch in the dark to turn off the transistor, a tense voice announced the death of Pope John XXIII.

She was so little prepared for it that she remained completely still and almost senseless under the blow, and then the magnitude of the loss carried away all her turmoil and her confusion and fears. She jumped out of bed. She had to tell him, she had to talk to him. She crossed the corridor, ran into his room, turned on the light and stood there, looking at him imploringly, tears streaming down her cheeks. He sat up in the bed, gaping, staring at her in astonishment.

– Lenny ... The Pope ...

The Pope, he thought. I must be going nuts.

– Pope John is dead.

Somehow he kept that grin from reaching his face. That's about the worst excuse I've ever heard, or will ever hear, he thought. You keep learning all the time. She sat down on the edge of the bed, looking at him so earnestly and in such distress, her hand was so cold when he touched it, and her shoulders were shaking so much, he had never felt so warm in his whole life.

I wish I were someone else, he thought. Poor kid.

– He was such a great man, such a good man. ....

I wish I were human, he thought. He never thought he would wish that someday. He wasn't going to hurt her, no matter what, you hurt a kid like that and the next thing you know you've started a relationship. He held her tight in his arms.

– Sure he was.

– It made all the difference in the world to be able to think about him, to know he was around. . . .

I hope she gets off that subject, he thought.

– Are you a Catholic, Lenny?

Jesus Christ, he thought. Am I now? I must be something. How am I to know what they did to me when I was a month old? I don't know what I am. I am, period. I just happened. I never liked any of it, so I must be a Catholic. Not that it meant anything.

– Please, Lenny, don't . . .

– I won't.

It's always like that. Crazy.

– Please . . .

Don't worry about a thing, kid. I'm a natural.

– Oh . . .

Easy, easy now. That's a good girl. She's made it. I've never been in love so much in my whole life, he thought. It may last me over the night, too. Love. You get an inch off the ground and call it flying. I'm sorry the old man dropped dead, he thought. Not that it means anything to me. He was still nothing but people. I must be a Catholic somewhere, even though they never told me. He seemed nicer than most, but so did Gary Cooper. No matter how high you look, you only get people. That's how bad it is.

She lay completely still, her eyes open and fixed, they always do. Physiology. It hits them real hard the first time, when it hits them right. Some don't get there for weeks and some don't get there at all, and become nymphomaniacs. You have to come across a nymphomaniac to really know what it's all about. It's all about goats.

He touched her arm.

– You okay?

She didn't answer and he saw that she was asleep. He had to laugh. It had hit her real hard, no kidding. Nature.

In the middle of the night he tried to open her arms gently but she woke up and pressed her arms tighter around him.

– Lenny.

– Yeah.

– How long will you be around?

– You don't have to worry. I never stick. I'm one of those roving birds. You won't have any trouble getting rid of me. No trouble at all.

– But I don't want to get rid of you.

She took his hand in the dark and held it. He couldn't go to sleep at all, holding hands like that. It was the funniest thing, finding himself like that with his hand in hers in the middle of nowhere. He had to laugh. You get a lucky break sometimes.

When she woke up again the hand was gone and in the

light of dawn she stared at the empty bed and the crumpled pillow, and only then she heard the alarm clock ringing on the bedside table, it went on and on, a cold, metallic indifference, a heartless statement of reality. She looked around, but his clothes were gone. She jumped out of bed and ran into the corridor. The bathroom was empty. Gone. She went back to his room and stood there a long while, then quickly made up the bed, she couldn't stand that gaping, wrinkled cynicism of pillows and sheets, it wasn't true, it wasn't like that at all, a cheap, superficial appearance of things that meant nothing and proved nothing at all, if you let your eyes take over, they can reduce almost anything to dirty laundry. You've got to have talent to look at reality. Creative looking.

What was he going to do, broke, alone, not even speaking the language, carrying his skis around in the middle of summer. What a pathetic jerk, running away like that out of sheer humility. Everything hits you at once. There'll be somebody else, there always is, that's why nothing is ever the same, and will never be. There was absolutely no one now. They'll elect a new Pope, of course, but it won't be the same thing at all. John XXIII had a human, earthly holiness, a glowing warmth of spirit and heart, that made all the difference in the world, and it had nothing to do with being an atheist. You can be an atheist and respect and love what is respectable and lovable. He didn't even give her a chance to make him a cup of coffee, a stray dog's humility. It isn't blasphemy even for a complete atheist, like me, to feel deeply

about a great human being like Pope John XXIII. I never
felt so lonely in my whole life. I could fall on my knees
in a church right now, and pray, simply as a tribute to him.
He never tried to convert anyone, he just was, and it was
enough, you knew somebody cared. You don't have to believe in God to believe in something. All the churches in the
world will look different now. He had done something
human to even the most inhuman-looking cathedrals, like
Chartres or Rheims, where faith had turned into cold stone
and was nothing but architecture, art. The human touch,
which is what God is about, after all. I don't feel guilty at
all, but I'm sure he would understand and forgive. Really,
I'm thinking like a practicing Catholic now. Besides, you
can perfectly well go into a church and pray without feeling
at all regressive. It's a release. And then, between sex, her
father, God, skis, and the utter misery of it all, she threw
herself on the bed and began to sob and sob, until she got
rid of some of it at least. Come on, Jess, in a way it's all
for the best. At least you've found out about yourself. From
now on, when you say no, you'll know it's not because you're
frigid but because it's important to you. I suppose I've done it
as a sort of protest against everything. The Berlin Wall
alone would be enough to make me do it. That's as good an
excuse as any, I guess. And I did have a crush on that guy.
I still have. I would probably let him do it again and again,
if only to make it all look less casual. It's all my fault. I
made him feel guilty so he went away. He can't be very far,
with his empty valise and his skis. That's right. Let's do

that. I'll find him and give him a lift to town. Smiling and cool, showing that there're no hard feelings. Poor bastard, he must feel damn awful. Men always do, afterward. He didn't know he was the first. I should have told him.

There was a note from her father on the living-room table and she glanced at it briefly. "Darling, I went to bed, come and have lunch with me tomorrow at the Chapeau Rouge, good news. . . ." She shoved it into her purse, ran out and jumped into the Sunbeam. There was something almost reproachful in the virginal whiteness of the orchard. It's ironic to be greeted by so much whiteness the morning after. Ha-ha-ha. In a fairytale the trees would be hanging their heads in shame and shedding their blossoms. She banged the door of the Sunbeam, started the car and caught sight of her scared, anguished face in the mirror: oh no, it simply can't be as bad as that. Nothing is. Come on, come on, Jess, get rid of your ego and slip into something more comfortable. Try wisdom. There might be a laugh there. Then she saw him sitting forlornly on his ridiculous suitcase on the side of the road, his head low, looking at his feet. She knew immediately what to do. Feminine instinct. Step on it and wave goodbye passing by. Superior and detached. That's my girl. That will really show him. She slowed down and stopped the car. He looked up.

Shook up. She's all shook up. Okay, I've tried. I've tried real hard. I've run away quiet, never mind the dough. I didn't want to use her after what happened. Now I have to go through with it. Fate, they say. Vocabulary. Well, it's her rotten luck, not mine. And there were some birds singing in the trees. And the orchards and the blue sky, and the air with the morning dew smelt honey sweet. The usual propaganda. Somebody up there is laughing. Someone that isn't even there, that's the biggest joke of all. She sat there in her car, looking at him.

– Why did you do that? Running away like that?

– A fellow's got to have manners.

– What kind of manners are those, Lenny?

– Well, I thought you'd rather wake up alone. Nice and proper.

– I know what I'm doing. I don't regret anything.

– Thanks.

– Why? Should I regret it? What's so important about it?

– I don't know.

Except that when nothing is important you get futility. Which is not so hot either.

– If that's the way you feel, no hard feelings, I mean, you could give me a lift into Geneva.

– What will you do in Geneva?

– I don't know. That's half the fun. I just like things to happen suddenly....

He looked at her and grinned.

– The way they do sometimes.

She didn't blush.

– Get in.

Now. Let's get on with the job. That's Angel over there, in the big black limousine. Watching. Suspicious bastard. Well, that's the way the cookie crumbles. He got up. First the skis. Then the suitcase. I wish she'd look away now. No sir. Can't take her eyes off little me. It'd take two men to lift that bloody stuff. He had to drag it and then he could almost feel her shocked eyes on the suitcase as he managed at last to lift it and throw it behind the seat. He straightened up. Their eyes met. Then she looked away. Jesus, smelled a rat. Me.

She didn't say a word to him all the way to the frontier. Kept staring ahead, which is a good thing after all, when you are driving. Sorry it had to end that way, kid. She'll probably tell the police, though. Almost wish she did. Quits.

– Don't they ever search your car?

No answer. Scorn. Keeps staring ahead like mad. Lenny's funeral. Now the Swiss side. Okay, it's okay. We're through. They didn't even bother to look at the CC plates. They sure know she won't do anything like that. That's Angel behind us again. I wish he'd get off my back.

– Where do you want me to drop you?

– The harbor will be fine. I know a fellow with a boat there. A luxury yacht. He told me they might need a deckhand, or something.

– Or something.

– You sure are sore at me, eh?

He caught her eyes on his face, in the mirror. Hard. But her voice was sure full of that stuff. Tears, they call it. Mass media.

– What's in the suitcase? Heroin? Gold? Yes, it's gold. Gold is very heavy.

– So what? Who cares?

– Nobody, I suppose. Only you didn't have to lay me for that. All you had to do was ask. I would have done it.

– That had nothing to do with it. Honestly.

– That's a new word for it.

– Listen, kid. A guy knows I'm starving, he makes an offer. The CC plates on your car, fellow Americans, all that. And he tells me there's some dough in it for me if I get you to take the suitcase across the frontier. So I do it. So what? That has nothing to do with you and me. It's them. It's their world. I don't care a damn what I do when I'm below six thousand feet and it's summer and no snow around. It's shit level here. You've got to conform.

– Yes, tell me that, Lenny. Tell me you're a rebel. It'll make me laugh. I could do with a laugh right now.

– I'm no rebel, Jess. That's the whole point. I don't care a damn. I don't care a damn about anything, except perhaps good snow.

And the way you look at me and feel about me right now. But I'll get over it. I can get over almost anything, including myself. That's how mean I am.

– I'm only a ski bum in summer, trying to survive. Not that I care much about living, you can have it. But I don't want to walk out on it either. Pride, I guess. I don't like life to lick me.

– You don't have to tell me, I've found out for myself. It's a pity, though. I sort of liked you. I suppose it's just because you're so good-looking. Get out.

She stopped the car. He stepped out, stood there, grinning, it's extraordinary how blond hair and good looks can make a face look innocent.

– It's that big black yacht over there. The *Cyprus*. In case you feel like it again.

She shrugged.

– Don't try so hard, Lenny. You're only human, after all.

– Why, thanks.

– I wish I could help you.

– Why don't you try? It could be fun.

– Goodbye, Lenny.

– Goodbye, kid. Don't try too hard, it's my turn to say it. You can't lick the world. There's just too much of it around.

She left him standing there, grinning, never to see him again.

8

IT WAS NOW ONLY SEVEN O'CLOCK AND SHE HAD
nowhere to go. The SPCA was open night and day but they
don't take care of humans there. Nobody does. Pope John
was dead. The Sunbeam was only a car. Her father would
understand, of course, but then he would understand almost
anything. And he might still need her, the strong, principled
girl, so there was no point in destroying the image. There
were several churches around, but she felt like talking to
someone. She drove around the harbor for a while. What a
pathetic bit of human flotsam. There would be a Jean Villon
lecture on French archaic poetry at nine o'clock at the
University. But she didn't feel like French archaic poetry
at all. Or rather, it was not that she didn't care for poetry,
she had a guilty feeling that poetry wouldn't care for her
right now. She hadn't even had time for a bath. She
stopped her car by the bridge, came down to the water and
stood still for a while, the light was cool and peaceful,
clean, even the seagulls were quiet. She had forgotten to
bring the bread to feed them, and so Lord Byron came,
waited, then swam away. Typical. It's all economics. You've

got to stop being so damn lyrical about everything, Jess. You don't have to become entirely realistic, only get rid of that lyrical puppy fat. Join the world. This is done through promiscuity. Sink. Once you reach the bottom, you'll be in. That's where the big party is on. Use sex, you'll meet the best people. Orgasm is progressive. It's funny how many bright, liberal people think of freedom in terms of sex. They even use sex for social protest. When you feel suicidal, pick up a fellow in the street: he'll do it for you and you'll get up from bed relieved and refreshed. Brand new. I don't think Marilyn really meant it. She was used to taking as many as twenty pills to sleep. Then a telephone call wakes her up, she can't go to sleep but she is dazed, she's forgotten she has already taken her dose and so she takes it again and it kills her. Lead a nonsensical life and then say life is absurd. Don't be lyrical or emotional: it's completely against the contemporary trend in literature. Be an exhibitionist, show everything in public, that's known as *not* being a phony. Don't sit broken-hearted looking at seagulls by the water's edge, it's bad literature. Seagulls, since Chekhov, have become such clichés it's surprising they can still fly. Beauty is a phony. Love is a *nebisch*. Get yourself fixed, kid. Freedom is a contraceptive. And you may get a Pulitzer in the bargain. Oh well, no use crying over spilt milk.

– Hey, Jess. W-w-we've been looking everywhere for y-y-you.

Jean was leaning over the railing, waving to her.

– We've been on a s-s-safari. We've got a fine trophy here. Look.

It was a big gray Rolls-Royce, with a middle-aged, suitably graying chauffeur in gray uniform. The chauffeur seemed worried. Paul was sitting in the back of the car, in a pose of nonchalant, debonair ease. His tie was undone and he looked ghastly. There was another man with him, sitting very erect in the corner, his hands crossed over a cane. He was wearing a Prince of Wales checked suit and a polka-dot tie, a canary waistcoat and a gray derby hat. His glassy blue eyes were bulging slightly out of their sockets, pushed from within by the rising level of booze. He was in such a state of alcoholic stupor it had an air of some human greatness about it. That at least was something no animal was capable of. You had to stop Darwin some-where, no matter what and no matter how. Jean sat next to the chauffeur, looking ghastly. They must have been at it all night, since they had heard the news. They were real buffs even though they were staunch atheists. Pope John had the highest popularity rating among the kids that year.

– We've got the Rolls and the chauffeur for twenty-four hours, Paul said. We stalked the beast as it was leaving the waterhole, the *Banque de Crédit Suisse,* and we shot him twice with my high-powered, double-barreled Polaroid. A Spanish gentleman, very suave. So he made a gentleman's agreement. He was gracious enough to lend us his Rolls and the chauffeur for twenty-four hours. Then we'll give him the negative.

– Aren't you going a little too far, fellows? It's almost like blackmail.

– Only a students' prank, Jess, only a students' prank. No social significance, good simple, clean fun. If you can't change the world, at least you can have some fun with it. Come on in. All leather. Animal skin. Thick hide, not like ours. Banks. Materialism. To hell with it. Why shouldn't we have some fun with materialism? Let's go for a drive, maybe it'll take us somewhere.

– You've been drinking.

– What the hell, it's still better than pouring gasoline over your head and setting yourself on fire, like in Vietnam. Mind you, I bet that will be the next craze among the kids. Setting themselves on fire in public places. Just for kicks. No social significance. I'll write to Lord Russell about it. Come on, let's go.

– I can't somehow quite see myself in a Rolls so early in the morning. I'd feel overdressed. What about class, anyway? There's a lecture on Russian lyrical poetry at ten o'clock.

– I think the Russians ought to wait before they talk lyrical poetry to the world. That's laying it on a bit thick. Get in.

The stiff in the back of the car didn't seem to breathe at all. Paul picked up a bottle of whiskey from the bar in front of the seat and put the mouth of the bottle to the man's lips, his Adam's apple jerked spasmodically as he gulped it down.

– What's that?

– That, as you say, is the baron. We found him sitting on a garbage can, waiting for the bar to open. He was sobering up, it was heartbreaking. Fortunately the Rolls has a built-in bar. We have probably saved his life. Quick action. You can't let a fellow sober up suddenly and face things. You've got to be merciful. Mind you, I'm not so sure it's booze that got him. I think it's neutrality. Swiss neutrality. Creeping Swiss neutrality, that's what it is. First your heart goes, then the brain. Then you become completely Swiss from head to foot: you've got total material security and you're completely neutral. You don't feel anything about anything any more. I wish I were an American Negro, at least they can think they've got something to live for. Chauffeur, drive on.

– Where shall I take you, sir?

– Don't ask any idiotic questions, just drive on. We are still young. We might still get somewhere.

– Very well, sir.

The baron's eyes were blue and glazed, his cheeks inflated, he seemed to hold back something, perhaps his laughter.

– Is he real?

– Got to be, or he wouldn't be drinking. It's such a beautiful Rolls-Royce, shall we drive it into the lake?

– L-l-let's do that, Jean said. That would r-really be p-prosperity.

– I beg your pardon, sir?

– Don't worry. We'll let you out first.

The baron hiccuped.

– He s-seems to like the idea, Jean said.

– Let's reward him with a drink.

Paul tilted the bottle against the baron's lips.

– What's eating us, kids? Jess asked.

– Nothing, Paul said. Very bad.

– Do you think Cardinal M-Montini will be elected? Jean asked.

– What time did you hear the news? Jess asked.

– Drive this car into the lake, I tell you.

– Sir! the chauffeur said.

– You English?

– Yes, sir.

– Then shut up. Build yourself an independent nuclear deterrent and shut up.

– It had n-nothing to do with him being the P-Pope, Jean said. He could have b-b-been an ice-cream vendor or a suspender s-salesman. You had to like him and that's all. R-religion had nothing to do with it.

– Get rid of this Rolls-Royce, do you hear me? We're patriots, don't you understand that? Swiss patriots. We're in the resistance movement. Switzerland has been invaded. It has been invaded by money. Our duty is to destroy the invader. We shall fight in the air and in the hills, we shall fight in the fields and on the beaches . . . we shall never surrender.

– You c-can't k-kill money, Jean said. The human s-s-soul is immortal.

– What's the matter, Jess? Why aren't you laughing?

– I've just had a bad accident, Paul.

– What happened?

– I've done it, you know.

You had to give it to the Rolls-Royce people, they certainly know how to make a silent car. Jean glanced at her. Maybe it'll cure him of stuttering, Jess thought. Shock treatment. He'll never stutter again. But he's too nice, nothing can cure the nice ones. They remain nice.

– How long have you known him?

Paul's voice was angry now and his face was white.

– I haven't known him at all.

– Oh, it was like that.

– Yes, it was like that. I told you. A bad accident.

– Chauffeur . . .

– Yes, sir?

– Drive us all into a tree. A hundred miles an hour. It's an order. You may jump out before.

– Very well, sir, but I shall not jump out.

– Paul, this is no laughing matter.

– Who's laughing?

– I don't understand myself how it happened.

– That's how it always happens. Who is he, anyway?

– A ski bum in summer. American. I've never seen any-one so lost in my whole life.

– That's how he played it, eh?

– Oh sh-shut up, Paul, Jean said. Shut up. It could have been w-worse. It could have been you, or even m-me.

– Driver, please take us back to Geneva.

– Thank you, mademoiselle.

– Jess.

– Yes, Paul?

– You were careful?

– No. Anything else you want to know?

– You stupid bitch.

– Leave her alone, Jean said.

– Now if you get pregnant I'll have to marry you, Paul said.

The baron was swaying gently in the back of the car. Paul threw the whiskey bottle through the window and buried his head in his hands.

–Oh God, he said. It's only a figure of speech, mind you. Jess stopped the car at the harbor.

– Please let me out here.

They both stared at her.

– You'll only get hurt, Paul said.

– That's the p-price of almost everything that's worth while, Jean said. G-g-go ahead, Jess.

– It's easy for you, Paul said. You never had a chance with her anyway.

–Y-yes I had, hadn't I, Jess?

–Maybe it will still be all right somehow, Jess said.

She found him in the cabin, sitting on the berth. He was holding his idiotic skis on his knees, polishing them. Caressing his skis, godammit. Sitting there in the middle of nowhere. How lost can you get? Rosebud, she thought suddenly. It's all Rosebud stuff, like in *Citizen Kane,* the best picture ever made. A sled called Rosebud that Citizen Kane loved when he was a child and that had been taken away from him and it marked him for life. It was all pure, undiluted Freud, you couldn't even feel mad at him or jealous. But I'm not going to mother him either. Only try to help, if I can. He's a mess. I've never seen anyone so confused, never.

He didn't even look up at her, kept polishing his skis. Full of hostility, I suppose.

Sex mad, he thought. I sure started something.

– I didn't think you'd come around, not so soon anyway.

– I only came to apologize.

That's a new name for it, he thought.

– What for?

– For being scornful and moralizing and self-righteous. I have no right to blame or despise anyone but myself.

Jesus Christ, he thought. She sure is full of it.

– You shouldn't have come in here, he said.

It's the eyes, she thought. The eyes are good. I'm absolutely positive there. He's only trying to conform, trying to fit in. Putting up a front. It's-a-tough-world-and-don't-give-me-that attitude. Fantastic insecurity. I have to be patient with him.

He put his skis down.

– You've got it all wrong, I guess. I didn't mean to lay you. It just happened. Some of the best things in life are like that. They just happen. That's the trouble with it. You can't even say it's all lousy, you can't bet on that. Just when you expect the worst, you get the best. No security. But I don't want any of it. I don't want me to happen to you and I don't want you to happen to me. Nobody hurt.

Now he's getting big brother about me. Protective. Sweet.

– But why, Lenny? Only as a matter of curiosity?

– I'll tell you why. It's all fine as long as you can take it or leave it. When you begin to care, you're a sitting duck. Everything becomes important. I like it with you. I like it a lot, but I don't want it to become something personal. Not even for a lousy twenty-four thousand bucks. Okay?

– Okay.

She sat down on the edge of the berth. He's scared of me. Doesn't trust himself. Poor guy. It's stronger than both of us, Lenny.

Maybe she'll do it for nothing now, he thought. Maybe she'll do it only for dough. It's a lot of dough, even half and half. But I've got to make sure. You can't trust her. You begin to think it's strictly on the level, fifty-fifty, you begin to feel safe and then she goes big on you and goes to the police and tells everything. Love.

– And I don't want to hurt you, either. I don't care enough about you. You've got to care to be mean. You sure make me talk a lot. It's because you make me nervous, I guess.

– You make me nervous too.

It was funny how American he looked. She never saw anyone looking more American in Geneva. He had no business being in Europe at all.

– When did you leave home, Lenny?

– What home?

– The States, I mean.

– About a year and a half ago.

– Why?

– I don't know why. Demography, I guess. There's too much of it back there, too much of everything. I've just fallen out. I'm just part of the population explosion, I guess.

There was a truly pathetic, ugly-duckling quality about him, except that he was terribly good-looking. Freckles. Look what happened to Huckleberry Finn. But I really have no right to feel superior or ironic.

She was sitting on the edge of the berth, like a rock. Stubborn bitch. You had to give her that.

– Sit down. Make yourself at home. But there's nothing here for hospitality. I can't even give you a cup of coffee.

– I don't want any. I only came here to take a good look at you, try to understand.

– Try to understand what? What's there to understand? Things just are.

– I don't know why I've done it.

– Oh, that. You were overdue.

Now she was looking at him like she had put something into her eyes. Full-eyed. Meaningful. Full of expression.

– Say, you aren't falling for me or anything?

– I don't know. Maybe.

– Well, don't. I'm real. That's not the stuff dreams are made of.

Hurt. She sure knows how to get it through to you. Considerate, I've got to play it considerate. Or next thing I know she'll go to the consulate with those CC plates of hers and have me kicked out of the country. They can get awfully mean when they have a crush on you.

– Listen, kid, you oughtn't to feel bad about it. It's got nothing to do with you. It's not personal. It could've been any girl, no matter who, Marilyn Monroe, it would still be the same. It's got nothing to do with you being you.

Hell, that didn't come out at all right. I give up. Who cares anyway?

– Lenny.

She hesitated a moment. They always do that for importance.

– Was I . . . bad?

– No, you were good. Don't get any crazy ideas. You were great. Any guy will tell you that. You don't have to worry about a thing.

– It all meant absolutely nothing to you.

Holy Moses!

– Wake up, kid, it's only me. I've told you I'm real.

I wish she'd get the hell out of here. Sitting there smiling like she knew better.

– I don't have it in me. You know something? I just wouldn't have anything to do with a girl who would fall for me.

– You really hate yourself, Lenny, don't you?

– No, no. I wouldn't say that. Why should I? I'm the same as anyone else, human. You can't blame yourself for that. We didn't vote on any of it, did we?

Some fucking democracy, he thought.

– There's more in life than skiing, you know.

– Maybe so, but it's not for me.

– I think I'd better go.

– Yeah, you better.

She got up from the berth at last.

– Goodbye, Lenny. You'll never see me again.

– Goodbye, Jess. No hard feelings. Happens all the time.

Jesus Christ. She sure don't give up easy.

She went out on the deck and stood there a moment looking at the hundreds of pleasure boats moored alongside. There is a gentle, pastel quality in the light over Geneva that you could easily mistake for sympathy, you can read meaning into almost anything. The water was pale gray and quiet. I'll get over it. It's only because he was the first and it worked. They say it never works the first time. But it did. You'd never have thought that a man could be so passionate and tender and careful without being in love. But he could. Technique. He had done his best and that was all. She had never met anyone she liked more. But he was right. You had to be modern about those things. She wandered around the harbor for a while, her textbooks under her arm, then remembered the lecture on Russian lyric poetry at ten o'clock and drove to the University and sat through the lecture smiling happily. When it was all over she stared at the word "Lenny" written a few hundred times on a sheet of paper and caught the intrigued expression on Chuck's face. Chuck was sitting next to her.

– What's the matter with you, Jess? You've got a new mysterious smile. What's the Greta Garbo act about?

– I've discovered the meaning of life.

– There isn't one. It was all an accident.

– That was last year, Chuck. This year the kids have a new fad. Life is loving.

– You got laid?

– Poor Chuck. You'll never know.

– You've got such an original mind, Jess. Life is loving, eh? Next thing you'll discover the greatness of maternity. Why don't you go write captions for *Vogue*?

– Stop feeling sorry for yourself, Chuck. We can't all be in love.

– A progressive girl like you should have slept with me long ago. It would have given you a considerable amount of ideological satisfaction. Sleeping with a Negro. You'd feel you were really doing something about it.

– You win.

It was now about one and she remembered her father's
note and drove to the Chapeau Rouge in an almost detached mood. I might even write a book about myself just
to show how detached I am. Anyway, it didn't look too
bad. He's broke, he doesn't speak the language, it's summer and there's no place where he can go, so there's no
reason at all to feel pessimistic about it. He's stuck here.

She parked the Sunbeam in front of the Chapeau Rouge
and went in. The restaurant was the chic-est thing in town.
They didn't even indicate the prices on the menu, that's
how chic they were. Only twenty tables, thick carpets, Klee,
Miró and even some Jan Lebensteins on the walls and all
the waiters wore tails. German Common Marketeers, Swiss
bankers, South American Ambassadors. The best call girls,
middle-aged, face-lifted, pearl-necklaced, calorie-counting
minks, talking of hysterectomies and Balenciaga, and that's
how she imagined the twenties, George Grosz cartoons,
Kurt Weill, Bertolt Brecht, *Im Westen nichts neues*. Brilliant. She smiled her way through gracefully, hello there,
holding her purse elegantly, while the maître d'hôtel led her
to her father's table in the best corner. Each table had a
status here, *Fräulein Else,* she thought. I remind myself of
Arthur Schnitzler's *Fräulein Else,* the only good novel he
wrote. Her father rose to greet her, the handsomest man
in the place. He always was.

– I'm glad you found my message.

– What's up?

– I've taken a job.

They both smiled: he didn't sound serious.

– Aren't you being rather reckless? What sort of a job?

– Export-import, that kind of thing. Initiative. Expense account.

He made a face.

– I'm scared stiff.

– You'll do it very well.

– Thank you. They said they needed my experience in dealing with foreign countries. Whatever that means.

– Swiss firm?

– Oh yes, very.

He took her hand and kissed it.

– Now you'll be able to finish your studies here.

– I'm not sure I want to. As a matter of fact I was thinking of taking a job myself.

– What kind of a job, Jess?

Smuggling gold from France into Switzerland.

– I don't quite know myself. Part time. Import-export, I suppose. It always is. Do we have to give up our CC plates immediately?

– No, not for a few weeks.

That should be enough, she thought. Two or three trips across the frontier, he had said. She withdrew her hand. It didn't look right, in a smart-ass joint like that, to hold hands with your father across the table. I'll do that for him as an act of love. Simply to prove that someone is willing to do something for him. That ought to shake him up a little.

Jess Donahue, the good Saint Bernard. I can't understand how he can have so much ego with so little feeling of identity. It's about the worst combination you can get. Maybe I'm not even in love with him. Maybe it's just that I need an excuse for having slept with him. I'm not going to cry, dammit. Not here.

– Jess! What's the matter?

– Only that I have a lover.

Or had.

He looked stricken. Stricken: that's how modern and broadminded he was. They were eating an omelet with white truffles.

– I thought I'd better be frank about it.

– Who is he?

– A ski bum in summer. American. One of those fall-outs. No good, let's face it.

– How can you be in love with someone you so obviously don't respect?

– I didn't say I was in love. I said I had a lover. Besides, I can. You should know that much about me.

– Yes, I know. But I'm your father. That makes it rather different.

– Now, really, I didn't mean that at all. Stop kicking yourself.

– How long have you known him?

No, she thought. I can't. I can't tell him that. It would sound too awful. It would sound too close to the bathroom.

– Oh, a few weeks. More or less.

– What's his background?

– I don't know. I didn't ask.

– Did you ask his name?

– Father, really. It's Lenny.

– Lenny, huh? Lenny what?

She shook her head. I wish I were dead.

– I don't know.

– Sounds like the real thing.

– Please.

– I mean it. If you didn't even think of asking his name, it must have been pretty overwhelming.

– It was. And still is.

– Oh.

– Am I being a bitch? Discussing it with you like this? Does it . . . does it hurt?

– No. There is, of course, one thing.

– What thing.

– I wish I had met you first.

She grabbed his hands.

– I love you, I love you, I love you. . . .

Tears like mad now. They are all looking, too. Fascinated. They never see anything except jewels here. Oh God, I do hate the bourgeoisie so.

– What am I to do?

– We ought to go back to the States.

– Not now.

– Is it as serious as that?

– Not now that you've got a good job, I mean.

– I see. Perhaps I ought to meet him then.

– I don't even know if I'll ever see him again myself.

– I can feel you've made up your mind, Jess. And you're a very strong-minded girl.

The ironic smile was back on his lips now. I don't even know if it's kindness, tolerance, understanding, or if he has been so crushed that he can take almost anything now. Except that his hair looks suddenly grayer to me, that's how guilty I feel. I, it's always I with me. I do hate myself so. All a ski bum wants is to get through the summer months somehow. He didn't even bother to lie to me. So rude. Oh God, I wish there were something else in life besides love.

– Let's not talk about it any more, please. Tell me more about your job.

– High finance. Millions of dollars. Guldens. Cruzeiros. Marks . . . All sorts of exotic, romantic names . . .

– Yes?

I'll go and do it. I've lost my virginity already, so what the hell. I'm going to smuggle that gold for him just to shake up his overconfidence. His absolute belief in nothing. I'll do it strictly on philosophical grounds. At least I'll know if I'm capable of love. Oh God, I really don't seem to be able to think of anything else but myself. Feudalism. The feudal little Kingdom of I again. How small can you get. One day I'll probably go and have four or five children just to have more of myself around.

9

THROUGH THE PORTHOLE YOU COULD SEE THE GULLS messing around and you could hear their sharp, stupid cries, noisy bastards, they always sound so damn sad. But they didn't mean it at all. Just the kind of voice they've got. It's all in your mind. You hear an ass cry, it's a happy ass, as happy as only an ass can be, and you hear it sad. Poor son of a bitch, you say to yourself. Self-pity. You go up the Scheidegg at night and you look at the stars and you feel good, you feel close to something and the stars aren't even there, they've been dead matter for ages. Just pretending. Nothing there.

He was lying on the berth, his hands crossed behind his neck. The berth was narrow. He could feel her body just as if it were his own. She lay naked and all gone, limp, one knee over his legs, holding on to him with both arms. Her hair was all over her face. It was soft and sweet and you could almost catch yourself imagining things. You almost wished there was more to it than there was or could be. That's how good it was with her.

She pressed herself closer against him, holding him

tighter in her arms, hugging him, her head resting against his shoulder, and lay very still and gentle again and it felt peaceful, quiet. He liked the quiet that went with it, once you had both done your bit, he liked that a lot. I'll remember it, he thought. I could stay like that forever except there's no such thing. You can't go on an eternity kick. It's all "nice to have met you."

– We go half and half, he said. That'll make twelve thousand each.

– I told you I don't want the money.

– Well, you'll have to take it, or you'll make me feel I'm using you.

– That's all right.

– Then we'll each go our own way. You don't have to worry. You'll never see me again.

– I'm not quite ready for that.

– For what?

– For not seeing you.

– Okay, take your time. Say when.

He stroked her hair gently. She sure is hung up on me, he thought. Serious, they always get serious about sex. Makes it respectable.

– Lenny, do you have a family?

– No thanks.

– No one?

– I guess if I hired a detective he'd find my mother someplace. But he'd have to look real hard. My father got himself killed somewhere funny.

– What do you mean, somewhere funny?

– Some crazy place, I can't even pronounce it. Geography, you know. My father got himself killed for geography. Chaos, Thaos.

– Laos.

– That's it. The places those guys go to get themselves killed, it's a real joke.

– You lived with him?

– No, I can't say that. I sort of knew him, that's all. Laos, that's it. I was trying to remember the other day. Not that it matters.

It was the funniest thing, they must've been here for hours, and it didn't feel like time at all. It felt like nothing he had ever known. You could almost believe it was there to stay, that's how funny it was.

There's something about her I'd like to keep, he thought. A picture, maybe. Some of those pictures can last you a lifetime, if you take good care of them. Maybe I ought to ask her.

But I have to watch it, he thought. I don't want anything to go important on me. Not for a lousy twelve thousand bucks.

– You don't have to go through with it.

– I don't mind.

– You should mind. It's breaking the law, after all. Don't tell me you approve of that.

– You don't have to feel guilty about it, Lenny. Just tell me you love me. That will do the trick all right. What's so funny?

– Remembered a friend of mine.

– What about him?

– Dick Brillianski, a trumpet player. He just never spoke at all. Thought all words were whores. But it was easy for him. He could say almost anything on his trumpet, and then it made sense. It sounded right.

– Why do you say that?

– You tell a girl "I love you," and it comes out like everybody was there, lying. You know what I mean?

– I think I do.

You say like "I love you" and you feel they've all been there before you and left their garbage. Vocabulary. Means nothing any more, like politics. But it makes a nice sound, sometimes.

– I love you, Lenny.

– From the diaphragm.

– What are you talking about?

– You have to say it from the diaphragm. That's a muscle in here. Real deep, not from the throat. I tried to be an actor once and that's the first thing they told me. That's when I quit. I just didn't have that much in my diaphragm.

– You're such a sweet bastard, Lenny.

– I'm not so sure about being sweet.

– Why do you need so much money, anyway?

– You live down here, you've got to breathe the air same as anyone else.

– But twenty-four thousand! That's a lot of air. Didn't they pay you enough for the first load we took across?

– Five hundred francs, that's how new I was. Didn't know a thing. Sounded like a lot of dough to me. But now they're talking. Twenty-four thousand dollars, they say. One trip across the frontier. That would make me really independent. I could go up there and get lost. No more skiing lessons. No more yes ma'am, no ma'am. It's particularly the yes ma'am that I don't care for. You ask any skiing instructor, he'll tell you what I'm talking about.

– I can imagine what you're talking about.

– You have to say yes ma'am lots of times if you want to keep hired without an instructor's license. That's one thing you don't need a license for in Switzerland.

– Do you always say yes ma'am, Lenny?

– Now you're talking, Jess. Comes right from the diaphragm, I can hear that. Don't be sore. I've told you I'm real. Sure, I've said yes ma'am now and again. Not always, mind you. Sometimes I'd rather go hungry. I seem to have the kind of looks they like when they pick a ski instructor.

– And you'd rather do that than work?

He didn't speak for quite a while. He didn't seem to have heard her.

– One time I didn't say yes ma'am, she went to her husband and told him I was trying to make her. Old trick, but they almost called the police. Mind you, I'm not blaming the bitch. She felt hurt. Fair enough. I don't bellyache about people, or anything. There's a lot of it I like. Give me a good stretch of snow, far and high enough, a clear night, no one around, and I get so high you can hear me. Honest, I even catch myself singing, that's how good I can feel. I'm not one of those guys who knock everything.

– What have they done to you, Lenny?

– What you talking about?

– You're maimed. Thwarted. They must have hurt you very badly.

– Nobody hurt me. No one hurt me or is going to. I don't stick around long enough for that. Never give them a chance.

Them.

– Perhaps you don't give them a chance to love you, either.

– Love, he said. Yes.

He fell silent for a moment.

– You talk big, Jess. I guess you don't even know how big you talk.

She got up from the berth. She felt even more naked than she was. Bare. Bare inside. She began to dress quietly.

That's right, kid, he thought. I'm not going to let you go big on me. I wish we were someone else, though, not you and me. They could've used it, I bet. Lots of guys don't ask for more, I guess. I wish I were one of them. I wish I didn't have what I have. Futility. It seems you don't have to have religion to catch that. I thought I could only catch fleas, but there you are. Tough shit. And I'm not going to hurt you, either. Not for a lousy twelve thousand bucks. Love. Jesus Christ, what kind of talk is that? I'm not a dog looking for a master, just a dog. There isn't a master around, anyway. Only people.

–Anything the matter, kid?

–Nothing. Time for me to go.

–Did I say something wrong?

–No, you were only honest.

–Gee, I'm sorry. I didn't mean to be.

She stared at him. I'd better remember what he looks like. After all, it was my first love.

–I wasn't going to do it for money.

–Now what on earth else would you do it for, Jess?

Now she's even ashamed to dress in front of me. That's how bad it is. You don't dress in front of a stranger.

–What else would you do it for, Jess? Tell me. Maybe we can get it for you.

–Goodbye, Lenny. I'm sorry I can't help you.

–You mean the CC plate?

–No, I didn't mean that.

–Well, you know where to find me if you change your mind.

He lay on his back, his eyes closed, smiling. It's the funniest thing, you can't even trust sex any more. It has a way of turning into something else. And then what? Then you become important to yourself. Life becomes important. The worst thing that can hit a guy. Like Abe Shaw had said in his famous *samurai* or *harakiri* or *kamikaze* or whatever those immortal pearls of oriental crap were called: "Don't fall in love unless you're already married with five children. Then you can; it will help you get away from your wife and kids." But it didn't work. Bruised all over. It'll take me a couple of days to get over it. Maybe longer. Maybe a lot longer. The bloody seagulls, he thought, they sure sound sorry for themselves.

10

THE RED BUTTON CAFÉ WAS THE BAN-THE-BOMB HEAD-
quarters and espresso shop. They had the best coffee in
town there and the latest records and books and they
were open twenty-four hours, night and day, like the
SPCA. You could always go there and get a nice moral lift,
a feeling of purpose, think of something bigger and more
important than yourself, and it took your mind off things.
The place was run somewhat on the lines of Alcoholics
Anonymous, you could go there and seek comfort and con-
solation, listening to a Bertrand Russell type of talk on an
impending nuclear doom of such cosmic magnitude that
your own little private hurt became utterly unimportant and
you could enjoy a peace of mind that made you feel refreshed and relieved, since the idea of God was no longer ac-
tive. Anybody could go there and sign the Ban-the-Bomb
Manifesto at any time, day or night. Not a moment wasted.
Khrushchev could press the button at any time and it was
important you should be able to do something about it at
any time too. Whenever a kid had a lousy love affair or got
pregnant, she always went to the Ban-the-Bomb head-

quarters just to get back her sense of proportion and remember what was really important. You could sit there
and think about overkill and you felt comforted, it would
all be taken care of. A tall, stooped student in a red-and-
black-checked shirt, Alain Rossay, who went to jail regularly for breaking the windows of the Soviet and American
embassies as a protest against Swiss neutrality, was serving
coffee at the espressso machine; the students worked on a
voluntary basis, in relays, two days a week.

– Hello, Jess.

– *Salut.*

She immediately noticed an air of excitement and ex-
pectation about the place. The Gennaro twins, who were
in her social science class, were listening to a German
student from Munich who was talking vehemently, his
glasses shining, his pink, babyish face looking particularly
babyish over a sparse, hard-won and unconvincing beard.
The jukebox was playing a Dave Brubeck piece. It's the
saxophone that does it, though, Jess thought. You take Paul
Desmond away and there's no more Dave Brubeck left. A
Dominican priest, the Reverend Father Bourre, affection-
ately referred to as R.F. or Babar, after the famous elephant,
was smoking an enormous briar pipe, next to Paul, and
there were the usual African students suffering from
racism in Russia and Bulgaria and one wall was covered
with a very good photograph of the mushroom cloud. The
Dominican priest was their favorite fall guy, the man they
all hated to love. He did look like a baby elephant, sweet.

He enjoyed immensely the punishment he received there. Perhaps it made him feel Christian. Supposedly he taught religious drama at Fribourg University, but they had smelt a rat long ago, even though he never made any direct religious propaganda, the Dominicans were the smartest field workers, everybody knew that. They supported the worker priests in France before Pius XII banned them and they had even come out in support of Teilhard de Chardin when the Jesuits, his own order, forbade him to publish. It was the Dominicans who had circulated his philosophical writings on mimeographed sheets. You didn't have to believe in God to respect them and find comfort in their company. Jean's face brightened as he saw Jess. But Paul didn't even bother to say hello. Maybe she did take him a little for granted, though the only thing she wished was that he would go and marry somebody else.

– I'm telling you, Kurt Bohl was saying, if tomorrow you get yourself a supranational Europe, I am willing to bet anything that you will also have a supranationalism that will be the greatest threat Europe has yet presented to the world. It will make today's nationalism look like baby talk. We are probably in the process of building ourselves a nice nightmare. Take a supranational craving for a supranational power under supranational Hitlers or Stalins, and you will get the seeds of a new supranational history that will scare the wits out of the world. I don't mean to say it will go and exterminate the Jews, like we did in Germany, or anything like that, but oh boy, that's all I'm willing to say. The only realistic solution is world government through the United Nations on a socialist basis, with each country granted only municipal power. What is the alternative?

– Sex, Paul said. Hello, Jess.

– Hello.

– Have you heard the fantastic news? It was on the radio, only a minute ago.

The R.F. was smoking his pipe thoughtfully. He had nice eyes. They had to be nice. It was part of his trade.

– They announced that with a certain type of crayfish sexual climax lasts twenty-four hours. Nonstop. How about that? That ought to take care of everything. The greatest bit of news since Einstein.

– I don't believe Nkrumah would go for that, one of the African students at the other end of the room was saying. Nor Ben Bela. The Bandong spirit is gone, let's face it.

– I don't feel the new wave has anything new to say, Alain Rossay was saying to a girl at the counter. He was making her an espresso. It's all form with them. Technique. But inside the technique it's the old story again. They can't do much for you. Take Marienbad, or take Truffaut, or take Godard—well, perhaps not Godard. It's all trick for trick's sake. Something you get an aesthetic kick from, but no moral or ideological uplift.

They had the best avant-garde *ciné club* at the University. That's one thing they had there.

– Twenty-four hours of uninterrupted bliss, one of the Gennaro twins said. We have got our answer. No more *vague à l'âme.* No more confused longing. Something positive.

– He's too thin, a student was saying at the next table. There was a picture of Ray Charles on the wall exactly over him. Jean XXIII was round and warm. The perfect father image. Montini is too thin. They'll never vote for him. Besides, he looks like a New York Jewish lawyer. He hasn't got the right image. They would find it difficult to sell. The world is not ready for a thin Pope.

The jukebox switched to a Françoise Hardy record. That was about as low as you could get. You had to be fourteen years old to enjoy that. Or maybe the guy that put it on was a joker.

– You're a reactionary, that's what you are, one of the Negro students was saying. That's what Black Muslims are, racists.

– A twenty-four-hour *coitus noninterruptus,* Paul said. That ought to wipe Switzerland off the map.

– I can't see what you fellows are so excited about, Kurt said. Who's a crayfish here? It only goes to show that man is a biological misfit, which is one thing we knew already.

– A great, beautiful thing like that, it brings tears to the eyes even to think about it, the Gennaro twin said. And who gets it? Some shrimp. That's God for you. R.F., you ought to be ashamed of yourself.

The R.F. puffed on his pipe.

– I can tell you, R.F., there are no atheists among them shrimps, Paul said.

– We ought to go to the United Nations with this, the Gennaro twin said. We ought to take it up with the Human Rights Commission. Take it away from the shrimps, I say. Give it to us human beings.

– That's a nice democratic platform, Paul said.

– No it isn't, Jean said. It w-won't work. Not with C-Catholics, n-n-not with Protestants, and not with C-C-Communists around.

– Besides, Paul said, if you go with this to the United Nations and get some action, all you will achieve is a massacre of crayfish. Remember the Congo.

– Anyway, the Russians will get there first, as always, the Gennaro twin said. They are raising their standard of living like mad. They'll beat us to it. They have the best scientific brains. And you know what? If Khrushchev achieves a twenty-four-hour orgasm we'll lose France and Italy to the Communists immediately.

– All we need is some more educated, idealistic scientists, Paul said. Better schools, more education. We'll get it from the crayfish all right. We must explain to our kids that there's a great, bright hope shining ahead, give them a purpose in life, a goal. They will study like mad. You've got to have confidence in human genius. I'm idealistic enough to believe that one day mankind will achieve twenty-four-hour-a-day bliss. I believe in human greatness. What about you, Jess?

– I'll be the umpire, Jess said. Come on, R.F., it's your turn.

The Dominican was emptying his pipe into the ashtray.

– You smoke too much, padre, Jess said.

– The more I listen to you young people, the R.F. said, the more convinced I become that we are due for a great religious revival.

– He calls that a religious revival, the Gennaro twin said. Mind you, there are sects in India who also have a mystical approach to sex.

The priest was carefully putting away his pipe and tobacco pouch under his cassock. He was wearing steel-rimmed glasses, and had very little hair left. Jess had always liked him. His trade had nothing to do with it.

– *Eh bien, mes enfants,* he said, I'm delighted that you young people are looking for something bigger than yourselves. As far as I am concerned, twenty-four hours is perhaps good for some lousy shrimp, but not good enough for me.

– Not good enough, eh? the Gennaro twin said. Of course, he's one of those eternity fiends. Eternal bliss. Exigent bastard.

– But then I would like to add something. . . .

He rubbed his rolypoly hands with obvious satisfaction.

– You look like a cat who is going to eat a few mice, Jess said.

– You'll have to excuse my English, please. Your generation is suffering from what for lack of a better word I shall call *over-debunk*. There was a lot of debunking that had to be done, of course. Bigotry, militarism, nationalism, religious intolerance, hypocrisy, phonyness, all sorts of dangerous, ready-made, artificially preserved false values. But your generation and the generation before yours went too far with their debunking job. You went overboard. Over-debunk, that's what you did. It's moral overkill. It's like those insecticides Rachel Carson speaks of in her book, that poison everything, and kill all the nice, useful bugs as well as the bad ones, and in the end poison human beings as well. In the end, it poisons life itself, the very air we breathe. That's what you did, morally and intellectually speaking. Yours is a silent spring. You have overprotected yourselves. You are all no more than twenty, twenty-two years old, but yours is a silent spring, I'm telling you. Nothing sings for you any more. You were so angry with all the dangerous, phony piper's tunes that you ended up by breaking all the pipes and hating all the tunes. You have reduced the world to a spiritual shambles. God is ha-ha-ha. The soul is ho-ho-ho. Booze is reality. Love is sex. Family—what's that, are you kidding? So all you have left now is the H-bomb. That at least gives you a purpose in life. To be against it, I mean. You've got something to live for, or to live against for, excuse my English again, but suppose the Russians and the Americans suddenly agree to get rid of the bomb? What then? You will be left with nothing.

– There will always be the Chinese, Kurt said gloomily.

– Did you ever have a girl, R.F.? the Gennaro twin asked.

– I did. Long before I thought of becoming a priest.

– And what did you think of it?

– Don't be an idiot, Paul said. He's become a priest. That's what he thought of it.

The Dominican rose from the table, smiling happily.

– I'm not running away from the battle, he said. But I'm going skiing tomorrow. Bernese Oberland. Summer runs. Seven thousand feet. No oxygen. Just like here with you young people. But I'm seeing some nice black sheep up there. At least, they think they are black. It will be fun. Before I go, however, I shall say one more word. . . .

– Oh, Godlessness! the Gennaro twin said.

– That's right, the Dominican said. Oh, Godlessness. But the point is: you don't seem to enjoy it. Something is still missing, eh? You got rid of God and, isn't that funny, something is still missing. Perhaps you ought to try to get rid of yourselves a little. Perhaps you will end up by getting rid of yourselves as well. I would begin by that, if I were you. We can always find room for novices in our monastery up in the Gral and there is good skiing there. We even have skiing brothers. I have a friend up there where I am going tomorrow, an American so-called writer, named Mr. Bug Moran. He keeps a sort of open-door hostel for American ski bums. I'm telling you this because he asked me a very interesting question the other day. A riddle, I think you call it in English. Yes, a riddle. You probably know it, it comes from some sort of American children's game. The question is: "Who took the cookie from the cookie jar?"

– "Not I took the cookie from the cookie jar," Jess said.

– "Then who took the cookie from the cookie jar?" Kurt said.

– Yes, the R.F. said, I see you know the game. Very interesting. You are all very bright and clever so maybe you'll find an answer. Who took the cookie from the cookie jar indeed. Well, maybe science did it, or maybe Freud did it, or maybe Marx did it. Or maybe prosperity, materialism. Hardboiled realism and rationalism. I don't know and I don't care. But you certainly seem to be missing the cookie very much. You twist and turn and ache looking for it. That's one way of admitting its existence, it seems to me. Well, goodnight, my sweet ones. I hope you'll reach happily a twenty-four-hour-a-day orgasm and thereby join the crayfish in the mud. I sincerely hope so. May you outshrimp the shrimp. Morally you are almost there already. It will take now only very little. I suggest a short cut, Communism or Fascism. And now if you'll excuse me . . .

He glided majestically from behind the table and out of the door, his wide robe flowing.

– Hey, don't be a moral prig, R.F., the Gennaro twin shouted after him. Pope John wasn't.

– He always tries to get the best of you, Kurt said. No humility at all.

They listened to a Miles Davis record on the jukebox. They are good at dialectics, Jess thought. You have to give that to them.

– Depressing bastard, Paul said.

She sat with them for a while, eating hardboiled eggs and drinking too much coffee, listening to their escapist talk, the civil rights march on Washington next month, the coming French atomic explosion in the Pacific, the Chinese threat to India, but nothing worked. It was one of those days when not even a nuclear war could do anything for you. What good is there in idealism if it doesn't help you to get over some minor problem?

– How do you become a hardboiled bitch, fellows? Maturity, I mean.

– You've got to have the right environment, the Gennaro twin said. A good, happy home, family affection, security. Then you're sure to make it. You become tough as hell. Without that all you can become is a misfit. Anybody can tell you that.

I should never have adopted that cheap tell-me-you-love-me-and-I'll-do-it-for-you attitude. No wonder he felt he was being used. Dammit, what kind of a writer can I expect to become if I don't even dare to break the law? I've had about all I can take from principles. They tend to be nothing but status symbols.

– You know what, fellows? I think I'm the youngest Grandma Moses around here. Bye.

Paul didn't even look up as she started to leave. She waited a moment, but he didn't. Some friend. She gave Jean a sweet, tragic smile, and he rose immediately.

– Sit down, Paul barked at him. Let her have her heartbreak. You can almost see her price go down. Then someone will be able to get her real cheap. Maybe even you, that's how cheap it might get.

– Shut up, Jean said.

– What's this interesting conversation about? the Gennaro twin asked.

– S-stop bleeding all over the t-t-table, Jean said.

– I think I'm going to have a fit of religious mania, Paul said. I've tried about everything else. To hell with you, Jess.

That made her feel a little better. She stayed on for a while, listening to "Sweet Georgia Brown."

– There's one thing you have to give Ray Charles, Paul said, there's simply no one else. No one at all. He's the one and only and there's no point in thinking there could be anyone else, ever.

She drove home slowly, feeling so miserable it was like losing the last illusions she could still have about herself. How private can you get? Nothing mattered but your personal little hurt. All these idealistic flights of generosity and indignation, the whole world a menacing, urgent, unsolved problem, hunger and injustice wherever you looked and here's Jess Donahue feeling suicidal because of a lousy love affair. Exquisite private sorrows blossoming behind the thick walls of the ugly little feudal Kingdom of I.

She found her father standing by the open window in the moonlight, a black coat thrown over his shoulders. Sober for almost two weeks now. There was more strength in him than she had credited him with. Stop judging your father, you brute. You either love him or go and join the matriarchy. Get rid of that hard core of femininity or you will end up with a prematurely dead husband and a stock majority.

– Hello, there. What are you doing? Cutting a romantic figure in the moonlight for your daughter's benefit?

– Wondering.

– I'm glad the moon still has it in her. I thought it had gone scientific, nothing but cold matter, like everything else. What are you wondering about, or are you just wondering?

– The nature of reality. I have received a letter from your mother. She offers to take us back. Or come back to us, if you prefer.

She stood speechless for a moment.

– *Ça, alors,* she said at last. The bottom must have fallen out of the Cadillac market.

– You're a little hard on her.

– Well, she was a little hard on us. But why, suddenly, out of the clear, blue sky . . .

– As a matter of fact, Jess, I had written to her.

– Oh yes.

– Yes. I told her that I was out of the service, an excellent job . . . with very good, almost immediate prospects. Exaggerating a bit. So . . .

He shook his head and laughed. But it didn't seem to hurt. It seemed almost gay. It was the first time in a long, long while that she was hearing him laugh simply because

something struck him as funny and not because something
struck him.

– The nature of reality. Money.

– Are you going to take her back?

– Oh no. I only wanted to be sure. It's part of my general
. . . sobering up. I'm taking a good, hard look around me.
Facts of life, that sort of thing.

– What are you planning to do, exactly?

– I've told you. No more escapism. Hardboiled materialism. I'm going to make money. There must be something about it. Some hidden charm. Let's try it, Jess. We've
never tried money, have we?

They laughed. She was always forgetting how young
and handsome he looked. A born charmer, he could have
even made a terrific diplomat if there hadn't been more
to him than charm. He has my nose and my chin, but the
eyes are a little darker. We are quite a pair. Two cosmo-
politans. So delightfully un-American. A strong dash of
Irishness. *Grands seigneurs*. Broke, but *chez* Givenchy.
Devil-may-care brinkmanship, that's about the only thing
we still have in common with the State Department's
foreign policy.

– We are going to conform. A villa in the South of
France. Picassos. Blue chips. Only the best.

And why not, why not? It was only Walter Mitty as
far as he was concerned, but she could do that for him.
She could still do something for someone, if only for her

own father. Half of twenty-four thousand dollars would be a good beginning.

– You see, Jess, I've come belatedly to a conclusion . . .

Except that I don't know where to find him. But he'll be back. I feel it in my bones. And he knows where to find me. Where the birds are. That about sums us all up.

– What conclusion?

– Humility. I've decided to become stinking rich. Who am I to refuse to stink?

– I can see you heading directly for a Trappist Monastery in that new Rolls-Royce, Father. Are we Catholics, by the way?

– Yes. Good Irish stock.

– I'm glad. That's always something to fall back on. Goodnight.

– Jess.

She looked down from the stairs. He was looking up at her, standing in the middle of the hall, his light black coat on his shoulders, his hands in his pockets. There was a dashing air about him that made her suddenly suspicious. Maybe a glass or two. But at least you couldn't tell, which was already a big progress.

– That fellow . . . How is it going?

– It isn't. The terrible thing about failing the first time is that you know there'll be other men and I find this . . . sad.

– Yes. Experience.

– I'm not quite ready for *that*.

– Sorry. I didn't mean to sound like a father.

– You feel "this is it," and the next thing you know you only had a lover. Oh well, I suppose you were right. It's all only Samson Delila and his Pussycats. Except that I'm not ready for that either. Goodnight.

– Goodnight.

She walked up to her room and crawled under the blanket. No matter how clever and worldly and chic you tried to be about it, it was all still there as authentic and real as before. I'll have to pick up my work at the SPCA again, at least I'll have the feeling I'm doing something about myself. I really begin to think that all I need is not La Rochefoucauld or Chamfort but a vet. The fair maiden behind the thick walls of the medieval little Kingdom of I and I suppose all the trumpets of Jericho were only jazz, Brad Chapski at the trumpet. I ought to try to think about myself in terms of light-years. Oh well, it's bad enough to be a lost puppy without being Einstein as well.

11

HE WENT FROM THE FREIHERR TO THE ALTE ON HIS
skis through the Zorn Pass and the Grundenthal and down
the Sturr in three days and two nights. They told him it
was a dangerous time of year to fool around the Grundenthal and they gave him every reason in the book for that:
you can't trust the snow there in July, with its soft under-
belly, it doesn't hold, the weight of your body can start
an avalanche, every year people get killed that way, what's
the matter with you, Lenny, you tired of living or something? Yeah, something, he thought. He wasn't half the
bastard he thought he was, that was the trouble. He was
still full of crap. The way he had suddenly felt protective
and important, holding her in his arms, was enough to
make you sick. You have to run in a case like that or the
next thing you know life begins to stick and you wake up
suddenly with a monkey on your back, a life addict. Love.
It's an old trick, like politics. Anything goes. Life always
tries to make sense to you. You've got to be real stupid to
fall for that. Even twenty-four thousand dollars weren't
worth it, you've got to protect yourself. I guess you can't

make a real bastard before you're thirty years of age. You've got to have maturity for that.

The fellows in Bug Moran's chalet had told him the snow in the Zorn Pass was so thick and heavy and so ready to slide you couldn't even break wind there without starting an avalanche. But he went all the same. He felt like it. Not like being killed, he didn't have that much crap in him, but he longed for the Thal with its twenty-mile, almost horizontal stretch of immaculate whiteness and silence and the feeling that no one had ever fouled up anyone or anything.

The R.F. went with him as far as the Grunden shelter, just for company. It was good to have the R.F. with you because he was such a jerk and so full of religion that he made you feel a real no-good and it gave you your strength back, sort of. The Dominican wasn't much of a skier and as they were halfway up the Grosse he was already panting heavily like an exhausted bear, his face red and his glasses clouded by his own breath.

– Stop panting, for Chrissake. You'll really start an avalanche.

– I'm having fun.

– Well, don't work so hard at it.

The Grosse Twins rose up on both sides, bright and glittering and you couldn't even see the snow, only light.

– What's the matter with you, Lenny? *Ça ne va pas?* You seem unhappy.

– I've got a bellyache.

About halfway to the Zorn, just above the tree line, they stopped for a meal of hot tea and sardines, squatting on the snow, watching the sun fall beyond the peak of the Schlagge where the Italian Bassano had vanished last year, trying to scale the son of a bitch, and the shadows came down on him suddenly from all sides like hungry birds. You never have more than three hours' sun in the Thal and then the shadows close in on you and you hear the ice cracking as the temperature goes down and the snow tightens and breaks. The Dominican lit his pipe, raising his eyes toward the heights. His plain, round face looked thoughtful. God. Cathedrals. Those bastards have got a one-track mind.

– What you thinking about?

– That my ass is frozen, the Dominican said. And that I'm running out of tobacco. I'm not a good man when my pipe is empty. Why are you laughing?

– Nothing. Let's go.

Now the Grosse Twins were gray, blue and green and the snow was getting rough and bitchy and the cold had its beak deep in you all the time and there was a kind of stillness around, a thick, frozen stillness that reached deep into your head and all the shit went out of you and you cared less and less, as if your life was happening to somebody else. He could still turn around and be back in Geneva tomorrow afternoon, not that he felt like it.

– Listen, Lenny, now it's not only my ass, my jewels are getting frozen too.

– What can a priest need his jewels for?

– Energy. That's where energy is stored.

He loved sardines. There was nothing like them. He laughed and shook his head.

– You know something funny? I've just turned down twenty-four thousand dollars in Geneva. How about that?

– Let's move on, *mon vieux,* the R.F. begged. Why did you turn them down?

– Too dangerous.

– Something dishonest?

– Oh, that's all right. But I got scared. There was a girl mixed up in it. I was beginning to fall for her. Crazy. No money is worth that. How can a fellow keep out of trouble if he begins to care? Jesus.

– He cared, the R.F. said.

– He sure did. Then look what happened. Okay, let's go.

They could see the Needle now at the other end of the Thal, pink with the invisible sun, and the Grunden shelter was now only two hours away and the sky was still blue but the stars were out already, winking, as they used to tell him when he was a kid. They can ruin you for life with their crap. They took good care not to tell you that most of them were dead and gone for millions of years. There was nothing there except cold matter. Come on, you bum, it's only sex and you can always get it wholesale. Never fall for something that's got more than sex in it. Any Chinese cookie can tell you that. He checked, leaned

over his poles, his head lowered, still trying to fight the
hook. The R.F. caught up with him.

– You can make the Grunden shelter alone?

– Of course. Why?

– Because I've got to go back.

– Back? *C'est fou!* You'll never make it in the dark.
You'll break a leg and freeze to death.

– Well, it's my ass.

– But what is it?

– I've changed my mind.

– Listen . . .

– I've just made up my mind I want those twenty-four
thousand dollars after all. I want them real bad.

– But, Lenny . . .

You always get rid of everything on a fast downhill
run and this was a long one, the longest in Switzerland.
For the first forty minutes he didn't even think of the silly
bitch, except once or twice maybe, if you could call that
thinking, only the eyes and the warmth, you had to keep
warm somehow. The best thing about skiing on a bright,
sparkling night like that is the stars, no matter how phony
they are. The way they are with you. Friendly. You have
fun with them, sort of. It's not very different from surf
riding, except you ride the night and not the ocean, and
it's the stars that are all over you and not the spray. You
feel it's your skis that are throwing snow up there into the
Milky Way. Galaxies. Nobody watches, so you can fool

around with them a little, like when you were a kid. It's great to look at them as long as you don't get the Enigma. Some bums he had known got the Enigma just from too much skiing alone among the stars and then religion set in, even the sky can get you, although there's nothing there. I've got to watch it with that girl, even though nothing that's got sex in it can be all bad. He slowed down and came to rest, breathing the cold, still air, took off his toque, rubbed his hair, then raised his eyes and grinned. Betelgeuse. He knew that one. It was personal between them, kind of. I bet you aren't even there, you old bitch. You always keep falling for something that isn't even there. But as long as you remember that, you're okay.

He reached the chalet after midnight on hard, mean snow with the dirt and rocks knocking at his knees and he went all shaky and lost more control on the last few miles than on all the run. He had to walk a mile carrying his skis. The first train was at 6 A.M. He didn't even know her phone number. He knew how to find the house, but the frontier was a problem. His passport was a week out of date now and he knew they wouldn't renew it for him. The last time he went to the consulate about it they even tried to keep it. Draft dodger, they said. They wanted him back. Angel could help fix that, but he didn't want to go through him, not now. He didn't want to be caught with his pants down, in love. Because that's what it would look like to a mean son of a bitch like Angel who didn't really know him.

They were all asleep at the chalet except Bug Moran and Genghis Cohn, who were still talking about what a phony reality was and how the Hindus had always known that, and there was a new bum he had never seen before, a kid from Norway, who made a living in summer as a pavement artist, painting the Crucifixion on sidewalks, except that he couldn't do that in Switzerland, because the Swiss are mad about keeping their streets clean. There was also Stan Nepobed, a deserter from the U.S. Air Force in Germany, who was on his way as a male nurse to a German nymphomaniac in Davos, and Malt Shapiro, who was also leaving his skis behind him at the chalet and was going to a Benedictine monastery in Ascona for three months to get baptized as a Christian, he always did that in summer, the monks fed him, so it was only nice manners after all. Bug Moran made him some coffee and cheese fondue, and how about going to the American Embassy in Berne to support the Negro march on Washington and break some windows?

– How about it, Lenny?

– I don't care much about Negroes. I don't think they're different.

He took a cup of coffee outside onto the terrace, it tasted better in the cold. The young bum from Norway followed him and they stood there drinking coffee and spitting into the night, which was the same as talking. The kid had long blond hair all over his shoulders looking like some teen-age Jesus Christ.

– Why d'you paint crucifixions all the time, pal?

– People like it. They pay to see it.

– Well, it does nothing for me. I always walk out of a movie when I see there's a crucifixion in it, I can't sit through it. I don't think I could have sat through even the real thing.

The kid wanted to go to America real badly, he told him. They had something there he had heard about called Pope art, some kind of new religious painting. He could make a living there in the summer as a pavement artist and ski all winter.

They spat for a while silently into the night.

– Why did you come to Switzerland, Lenny?

– They told me they had the best snow and the best neutrality here. Like what I was looking for.

– How did you pay your fare?

– I can always make money in a pinch.

The kid looked at him respectfully.

– Holdup?

– Christ, no. That's kind of taking things too seriously. I never felt that serious about money or anything. You might have to kill a guy or a cop and you really have to care to do that.

– Then how?

Oh shit, Lenny thought. He was ruining the stars for him. I'm going to let him have it, he thought. Hero worship type.

– Well, I met a guy back there in New York. I posed for him.

– Was he an artist?

– Yeah, I suppose you can call him that. Photographer. I said okay, why not? Mind you, they were really putting the heat on you back home then. Cuba. Russia. Missiles. Demography. Vocabulary. Don't ask what your country can do for you, ask what you can do for your country. . . . They really were after your ass. So I did it. Expressing myself, sort of.

– What did you do?

– Pornography. Pornographic pictures. Three girls and me. I sent a postcard to everyone I could think of. The White House. The draft board. The Olympics team. Just telling them. But I don't feel like that any more. Maybe the Swiss air. Maybe neutrality. But you never know. I still have a few postcards left. It's a good document. Helps you to keep out of things. The last time they called me in, at the American Consulate, because of this draft business, I showed them a postcard or two. Figured they couldn't ask me to join the team after that. Moral turpitude. You can get out of almost anything on that ground. Remember that if you go to America. It's legal. I sure felt it ought to disqualify me from serving in the American Army all right. It's a great clean army.

– That's terrific, the kid said. And it worked?

– They said they would forward it through channels. Red tape. I haven't heard from them since, so I guess it worked.

It was a lie, but you had to work at your image, what the hell? And this was a new kid and he had to give him something to think about. He liked the way he was looking at him after that, respectfully, kind of. Big brother. He felt so lousy he had to impress someone, no matter whom. And it was great stuff. He meant it, too. Maybe the kid would do it someday. You had to pass down the great Olympic Flame. It was the funniest thing, the way he was looking at you now, like you were the champ. Hero worship. Three girls, too. He had to laugh.

– Goodnight, pal. See you someday.

He was in Geneva late in the afternoon next day and he went to the SPCA to look for her, but she wasn't there and the Swiss vet, who was handling a hysterical poodle, told him in French something like get the hell out of here. Real mean. Anti-American.

– Will you tell Jess I was here?

– Can't you see this animal is suffering? the vet asked in English. The poodle was sure getting a lot of attention. Fancy pants, he thought.

– You tell her I was here, he told the vet. I don't care, but it must be something important, she's been looking for me everywhere.

They sure made you feel you weren't a dog in there.

He slept on the boat and spent the next day hanging around the SPCA clinic, and the next day again, and the next, but she didn't show up. He felt sick. He didn't quite know what it was. It felt like flu and a bellyache except there was no pain. The Negro whore put him up in her room above Angel's striptease joint and he stayed holed up there trying to get rid of the bug. The things that can hit you. Angel came up to see him, looking at him as if he knew something. Wearing a black camel-hair coat and a black camel-hair hat, and it was hot July, so it had to be for personality. He sure had an Arab face too. Sharp, knife-like. It's all in the nose with them.

– You want a shot of penicillin?

– I'll be okay.

– How's the girl coming along? I've got to know.

– What girl? Oh, that one. I haven't looked her up.

– Well, you've had your chance. Now we've got someone else.

– She was going to do it for me. Then I got the fucking bug.

– Sure, sure. Maybe you Americans are not so good in bed like us Arabs, eh?

– Ask your girl friend, that Negro kid. She'll tell you about me.

But he renewed his passport for him, just in case. Forged it. They can forge almost anything for you here.

The Negro girl brought him hot soups between acts, sitting on his bed, but he couldn't work up an interest.

– You feel real bad, sonny?

– Aw, maybe it's luck. Keeps me out of trouble. That crazy kid I told you about, remember?

– Yeah.

– She's mad about me. Keeps looking for me everywhere. Drives me nuts.

– Yeah.

But he didn't like the look she gave him. The old Methuselah look the Negroes have about them, like they've seen it all before they were born.

Then he went to the SPCA again and hung around a whole day and just as he was going to give up he saw her pull in in her car and go into the clinic, and he didn't stop her, he didn't want to take it away from some lousy dog. He had to wait for two hours. Then she came out and saw him and it still worked on her, you could see that at once.

They didn't speak for a year or so, just standing there, staring at each other, swallowing hard, it was the funniest thing you ever saw.

– I didn't know where to look for you, Jess.

– I told you, where the birds are.

I've been practically living there for the last five days, dammit.

– You work here every day?

– No, only twice a week.

– What d'you do that for?

– It helps.

– When I was a kid I thought I'd become a vet. A vet is really independent, no matter what or where. He can always take care of himself.

– Where are your skis, Lenny? Don't tell me you left them behind somewhere, I might think you were growing up. Why did you come back, anyway?

You could hear the dogs barking and whining back in there. They sure expressed themselves.

– I forgot the key, he said.

– What key?

– I forgot to give you the key to the boat, Jess. In case you felt like being alone in there. Don't be mad at me.

– You look sick.

– I've got double pneumonia.

– Lenny!

– Yes, the doctor said. They almost took me to the hospital. The doctor said I've got complications too. Everything. They even took my temperature, that's how bad it is.

– For God's sake, Lenny, you shouldn't be here. You should be in bed. . . .

– Yeah, I should be in bed, they all said that. Complications, you can die of it. It's okay, I don't mind, but I wanted to see you one last time before I go.

That ought to go down all right, he thought, you can't miss there. It ought to make everything nice again. You must always take the short cut. Now you don't have to lie to her. You don't have to give her all the crap about how sorry you were, how much you missed her, how you came back because you couldn't live without her. She looks all shook up. Tears in her eyes. She's got lovely eyes. It's the funniest thing, I've never felt better in my life, all of a sudden.

– Please, Lenny, don't stand there, let me drive you. . . .

– No, no, I'll be all right. I don't want you to do anything for me. I just thought I'd tell you. They'll give me a shot of something and I'll be all right. Here, take the key. Maybe tomorrow, or the next day. I'll shake it off. I can shake off almost anything.

She took the key and he walked away. He could hear the other dogs barking inside, furious, but this is a democracy. He turned back once and she still stood there, looking after him, so he walked a little unsteadily, the way you walk when you have double pneumonia with complications. He felt great, he had his overconfidence back now. The good thing about being a fink is that it gives you back your self-respect. A man has got to have that, you can't be a kid all your life.

12

THEY'VE FOUND A NAME FOR IT. A CYNICAL, BEASTLY, defeatist name. They call it "first love." They don't even try to discourage you, they are so damn sure you'll find out soon enough all by yourself. They put it down to experience. Their patronizing smiles suggest some stinking, clammy intimacy with the nature of things, with the facts of life, dust, ashes and the pursuit of wind. Even the kids at the University had a nice word for you: "Jess Donahue has been laid." They were twenty-one, twenty-two years old and so there was nothing they didn't know. You felt like telling them that no one, but no one, had ever been in love before you, you were making history. True, some immortal poetry had been written on the subject, but it was merely prophetic. The only trouble is, you can't turn happiness into a way of life, no one has ever succeeded in doing that. A moored boat in the harbor of Geneva is not the most secure place for Eternity. It was all like something that had fallen out of a nest when you were a kid, except that there was no nest. There had never been one, probably, only religious propaganda. She did sometimes pray for it to last forever. But it was only a release.

– What do you do when I'm not here, Lenny?

– You're always with me, Jess. The minute you're gone you fill the place.

He had to give her that, she was asking for it, but the funny thing was it wasn't a joke, either. Usually he could get rid of almost anything in bed, but something was wrong this time, it wasn't quite working that way. He would do it all again and again, but somehow he couldn't get rid of her. It was the first time sex was letting him down.

– What are you going to do, Lenny?

– Maybe we'll get over it.

– I love you, Lenny.

– I was going to say that myself, Jess. I almost said that.

– I love you with all my heart.

– Well, as long as we both know it, we'll be all right, I guess.

It's in the bag, he thought. She'll do it for me now, she's got motivation. But he couldn't bring himself to ask her. Not for a lousy twenty-four thousand bucks. It was worth more. No good selling yourself short. You've got hold of something real big this time. You'll never get anything bigger, it's the biggest thing you can get here. Jesus Christ, he thought, it exists. It's there all right. He laughed. He had to laugh.

– What's so funny?

– The way I feel about you, Jess, I could find myself looking for a job tomorrow.

– What's so terrible about that?

– Come on, kid, have a heart.

– What's so scary about getting a job, Lenny?

– I don't want to get social, that's what.

He spat through the porthole into the night. Stars again. Pretending. Forget it. They ain't there. It's all dead matter. Materialism. Science took care of them long ago.

– There's just too much of it around.

– Too much of what?

– Everything. Sometimes you get ashamed and sometimes you get mad. And sometimes you get social and try to change things. Crazy. Because there's no one around to help you. No one big enough, that is. Only people.

It was quite dark now. He couldn't even see her, so he could talk: he didn't mind so much in the dark.

– It's not blessed, sort of.

– What isn't?

– Aw, I don't know. Nothing is. It isn't taken care of, that's what I mean. You get no protection down here, all you can get is social security. Medicare.

He remembered that fat pig Bug Moran in his dirty sheepskin and his round queer's face looking like what he was always dreaming about only with glasses on, asking him, as he was preparing for a night trek across the Thal: "What's the matter, Lenny? Are you trying to walk out on it and move into something spiritual on your skis?"

He spat through the porthole again.

– How come there was no one before me, Jess?

– Because there was no one before you. It's as simple as that.

She pressed her head gently against his face, holding

him in her arms, and he felt the warm glow of her cheek against his lips, and his diaphragm began to beat faster again. Physiology, you can't help that.

– You take care of yourself?

– What does that mean?

– You can buy it in any drugstore here. It's legal. I wouldn't like to hurt you.

– I don't want to discuss that.

– Why not? You've got to be realistic about it. Reality, you can't lick that. It's here to stay. You ought to make sure. We don't want demography to set in.

– I don't mind a bit getting pregnant, Lenny.

– Now, Jess, you don't have to say that to get rid of me, I've told you. Just say when.

– Thanks.

– I mean it, kid. You don't have to scare me away.

– You're such a dog, Lenny. What's so terrible about bringing a child into the world?

– I told you, I don't like to hurt anyone. Why should I do that to my own kid? That's what's wrong about it. You sure think I'm made of stone or something. I don't want to worry my ass off. What kind of deal is that? Being born, I mean. You can have a good time without some poor kid paying for it.

He couldn't see her face in the dark, but she felt a little stiff in his arms, the way people are when they get hostility. He didn't want that. The only thing he was trying to do was not to hurt her or some lousy, innocent kid. He didn't need the dough that badly. And it was no use getting hurt, either. But he didn't like the way she was listening to him. Psychology. She was sure full of it.

– How come you drifted so far away from home, Lenny?

He lay silent for a while.

– America, he said.

He laughed.

– It's a pretty big country, Jess. Two hundred million, they say, and there I believe them. I don't want the responsibility.

– You mean politics?

– Hell, no. I don't bother with that. But you feel it's your country in a way, and they make you feel lousy. Take the Negroes. Now what do I care about Negroes? They're the same as anyone else. Screw them. Back home Negroes used to drive me nuts because of the way they were treated. I tell you, I don't want any of it. I guess I've got a thick skin. That's what's so great about Switzerland. They've got the best snow and the best neutrality here. You've got to do something about problems. You've got to do something about problems you can't do anything about. You've got to protect yourself. That's what human life is about, if you've got to be human. So I came over. I don't give a damn about Switzerland and I don't speak the language, so I feel fine here.

It ought to go down well, the Negro bit. Maybe I ought to tell her my father dropped the bomb on Sukiyaki or whatever that place was in Japan. That would make sense to her. She'd think I've got motivation. Stupid bitch. How come you drifted so far away from home, Lenny? Because they've got the best nothing in Switzerland, that's why. Jesus Christ.

It was the funniest thing, the way he thought Jesus Christ all the time, he was still full of vocabulary. You get thirsty, you ask for a Coke, without ever thinking. That's what mass media do to you. It's all gone subliminal. You go God or Jesus Christ all the time without even realizing it, even though you had never looked for help from someone that wasn't there in the first place.

She was learning quickly and she was damn good at it, she would do it all, and yet you didn't resent it, somehow. You couldn't tell what it was that made it so different and you even caught yourself taking her hand and kissing it and then holding it in yours against you and you had to laugh, it was the only trick you'd never done with a girl before. You could almost believe the cookie was still there, like when you were a kid. And not some crummy Chinese cookie with a crummy pearl of oriental phonyness in it, but the real thing, like there was one. You had to watch it all the time. Before you know you can become important to yourself. You begin to feel you're something special and then you think there's someone special watching over you and it all suddenly begins to make sense and you really start believing in it all, God, family, country, home, you really begin kidding yourself, like when you get maturity.

He pressed his hand against her breast, closing his eyes

so he could feel her better, kissing her and making the time go slow, as slow as he knew how. Jesus Christ, he thought, maybe it exists after all. Maybe the cookie is out there some place, and it crumbles down, sort of, and some of it reaches you. Bits of it. Crumbs. Particles. They only feed you crumbs here, the way they feed birds. But maybe there's a lot more of it some place. Love, they say. I'm going to tell her. You can tell the truth once, you've got to have humility.

– It's the best sex I've ever had, Jess, I mean it.

– I love you too, Lenny.

He woke up twice during the night and each time it was still there. You didn't mind a bit washing cars or driving trucks or going back home and doing your stretch in the army, as long as it was there and everything made sense. Motivation. You've got to have motivation. When you've got that you've got everything.

She was asleep in his arms and he kissed her and pulled her closer and then took her arms gently and put them around his neck, and pressed his cheek against her neck. Sex, he thought. There's nothing better.

He was down to his last ten francs now and it was no use asking Angel for an advance, the fink knew there was no future in it, that the girl wouldn't do it although he was no longer asking her. You could see the way that son of a bitch was looking at you that he smelt a rat, or maybe the Negro whore had tipped him off. You're in love, sonny, she'd told him. She told him so to his face, like that, she even let him have fifty francs on it. She sure believed in all that jukebox crap. All whores do. Love. What next. He wasn't going to fall for that. He wasn't going to fall for anything that's got a time element built in. He didn't want to be a loser. A loser, that's what you become the moment you let life get important on you. I've got lucidity.

But then he caught himself looking for a job in the *Herald Tribune* ads and he knew he had to watch it. You can become an addict. He didn't mind her so much when she was there, but when she was gone he sure resented her. Waiting for her. Just lying there and thinking about her all the time and hating the time. Slow bastard. He'd never felt about time like this before.

He could always write to that guy and tell him he was willing to make the American Olympic team, and go home and even take her with him, even though it meant all the mass media on your back again, the Negroes, the Whites, peace, war, economics, don't ask what your country can do for you, money. Jesus Christ, I don't want to feel human, I don't even like to speak the language.

She wasn't going to the SPCA any more. It made him laugh. He was taking it away from some cat or dog or canary, getting their share. Well, they were all classy dogs in there so it served them bloody right. Poodles. There are no strays in Switzerland.

She tried to give him some dough but he knew better than that. She still had those CC plates on her car. But not a word, nothing. That's how sentimental she was. It suited him fine, he didn't want her to do it for him anyway. It made everything platonic between them, sort of. And he didn't want to develop gratitude, anyway. It was scary enough to feel the way he did when he touched her hair or held her hand, looking at her, it was like not caring a damn about anything else. You could almost face the mass media, that's how he felt about her. She made him laugh, though. She took it all so damn seriously, he had to laugh.

– You look like it was the most important thing in your life.

– Perhaps it is. Or could be.

– Sure, maybe we could really make it together, a month or two, maybe. Then what? Okay, three months. A year. Then what? There ain't no such thing.

– What thing?

– You know. Eternity. Nobody watching. You've got pretty hair.

– Thanks.

– Pretty everything. You can't go on an eternity kick. You've got to kiss your ass goodbye, sooner or later.

She looked at him kind of nice, sad and a little hurt and then all of a sudden she asked him the funniest thing.

– What did they do to you, Lenny?

– How's that again?

– You've been robbed. You're so smart you let them take everything away from you. You're a sucker. You've let them rob you and you don't even know it. All you have left is your smart bare ass.

– Gee, now you're talking. That's all we've got all right and maybe it's too much to carry around already.

– It's all snow, huh?

– It sure is. It's all snow except that some of it's dirty.

– Why are you sticking around then?

– Curiosity. And then you get a good break sometimes, like you and me.

Then Angel gave up on him and took the key of the boat away from him and he had to break the lock.

– I'll have to find a room pretty soon. A place to live.

– You could come and stay with us.

– You kidding?

– Why should I?

– What about your father?

– What about him?

– You can't do that.

– Why not?

– I don't know.

He shook his head.

– A place to live, he said. What d'you know? I never thought I'd be looking for that someday.

– What about that smuggling job?

He almost stopped breathing. He couldn't believe she'd said that. He lay still a moment, waiting. You had to be sure about a thing like that.

– What about that smuggling job, Lenny?

It was like the best moment of his life. He felt suddenly so full of corn he almost couldn't hold it back any more.

– Oh, that. They've found a guy.

– Who?

– I don't know. Plenty of good will around.

– I'm sorry.

– It's okay. Maybe there'll be another chance. I'll let you know.

She was ready to do it for him. Sex. That's how big it can get. She had to have motivation, that's all.

– I'll let you know, Jess, he said.

His throat felt tight and something was wrong with his eyes. He didn't know it was so important to him. He didn't know he cared about money so much.

13

HE HAD A LIGHT BROWN, GOLDEN SKIN FROM SKIING
bare-chested in the sun and the eyes were dark green and
funny and there was no question that the world was beginning to look a great deal less unhappy than it used to. You
were very careful to show the kids that you still cared, that
your social consciousness was still in the right place, you
had to keep some sort of face, you discussed the chances of
Montini and the Modern Jazz Quartet and listened approvingly to their denunciation of Our-Cuba-and-South-Viet-
nam-Policies and the murder-of-the-American-Dream, even
though you felt all the time that as far as you were concerned the American dream was fine, just fine, never better.

She went to the SPCA once or twice, but even the vet
could see that she didn't need it any more. Anyway, the
most truthful answer she had ever heard was from the man
someone asked if he loved dogs, and he said, "No I love *a*
dog." But it was all so short, so desperately short. In Lenny's
own words, you couldn't go on an eternity kick. Of all the
cheap, mean tricks you could play on love, life's span was
about the meanest. The Ecumenical Council in Rome should

take this up, they should do something about it. There should be more to love than life. You felt rejected on grounds of mortality. You didn't believe in God so strongly you could almost feel the majestic absence beside you.

– Jess, hey, Jess.

– What is it, Paul?

– You have company, Jean and me. The year is nineteen sixty-three. This place here is called the earth, remember? You used to walk on it. Is there anything we can do to make you feel less happy?

– Paul, please stop suffering while you are driving.

– We have an old medieval French word for guys like him. *Gannef.* Archaic, thirteenth-century French. Means thief. Love. How cheap can you get?

– W . . . w . . . w . . .

– Are you trying to say something?

– W-w-what else is there? Jean asked.

– Wait a moment, here is a policeman. Let's ask him. There's nothing like an authoritative opinion.

It took him a hundred yards of screaming brakes to stop the car and the cop had a word or two to say about it.

– *Monsieur l'agent,* do you believe in love?

– You can get twenty days in jail for that, the cop told him.

– Do you believe in love?

– For insulting the Swiss police, the cop said.

– Paul, you are mad, Jess said.

– *Monsieur l'agent,* I wish to lodge a formal protest.

There is absolutely nothing else worth while in life and some American tramp is taking it all away from me. . . .

– F-f-from us, Jean said.

– Kids, please.

They had to drive to the police station for the alcohol test, where Paul shouted to the commissaire, "Can't you see we've lost our way in the materialistic wilderness?" and the commissaire said sedately, "There is a von Karajan concert tonight, we have museums and a high standard of spiritual life in Switzerland," and it was perfectly true, there were spiritual values everywhere, symphonies, art galleries, Europe was swarming with culture, *cul* culture, as Paul pointed out to them on their way home from the police station, with Jean driving very carefully. The fact was that nobody aged twenty could talk about God seriously any more, you had to pay for having had an education. But no one had managed to debunk culture yet and as long as there would be museums around no longing of the human soul would be left unfulfilled. Paul's father had twenty-five Picassos hanging on his walls, such was his craving for immortality. The human soul is crying out loud for more and more Picassos. Man doesn't live by sex alone. God is Art, Malraux almost said as much in his *Voices of Silence*. The Western World has licked all the material problems, we can now attend to the spiritual cravings of our soul and that's why Picasso commands such high prices today. They know he is holy. Spiritual values are the best investment today, you can't go wrong with a Jackson Pollock. Then Paul said, "Ah, wilder-

ness," a good title for a novel, except that it was already
taken, and Jean drove slowly around Geneva and along the
the lake with the first beautiful neon signs of Omega and
Nestlé and Movado and Fly Swissair glowing promisingly
and mysteriously in the darkening sky. Then they took
her to the harbor, where she had left her car, and there was
no point going to the boat, he wouldn't be there, he had
told her he had to see a friend and they had agreed to skip
it that afternoon. They were getting raw, anyway, both of
them. She walked onto the boat all the same and down
into the cabin, she only wanted to meditate, it didn't have
to be a cathedral. She found him sitting on the berth, waiting for her.

– I knew you wouldn't be here, Lenny.

– Yeah, like I knew you weren't coming.

It was the longest night they had spent together, not a
whole night but the better part of it, the part that wasn't
sleeping.

– Jess.

– Yes, Lenny?

– You're so quiet I'm missing you.

He missed her more and more, even when she was with
him. There was a lot of room around and she couldn't fill
it all, she was only human. He was holding her in his
arms and feeling her warm nakedness all over his and yet
he was missing her so bad it wasn't even funny. He felt like
something you couldn't reach with your body at all. It took
you only that far and it wasn't far at all. Jesus, maybe I'm

getting impotent, maybe I'm no longer good at it. But it wasn't that, it wasn't physiology at all. Maybe science will do something about it someday, some sort of transplant like they do with kidneys. They'll invent something different, a new organ, sort of, and graft it onto you so you could go all the way where sex couldn't take you at all. They do all sorts of things now. We need some new kind of transplant, sex has been around a long time and you felt you were ready to move on to something bigger, except you didn't have the right equipment. There's still a lot that science can do for you.

– Did you go to see your friend?

– No.

He hadn't been near Angel for more than a week now. Somehow he hadn't come around to it. With twenty-four thousand dollars you could get a lot of things. Maybe a dog. He had always wanted a dog. None of the fancy classy stuff, just a down-to-earth four-legged dog, preferably a stray, strays always know how to look after themselves, they don't bother you with affection. If they had kids, he would put them on skis as soon as they got legs, so that they knew what life was about. It scared the shit out of him merely to think about it. Maybe that's why he didn't dare to see Angel any more. There's nothing like knowing your own mind. She was playing with his hair now, like he was a kid. You couldn't help feeling sorry for her, she was so mixed up she didn't know what it was all about. She was so full of corn you felt like staying with her for keeps and trying to protect her, that's how stupid she was.

He was asleep now and it was nice to have him all to herself. When he was awake you always had an uneasy feeling that he had a life of his own, another relationship, in fact. But when he was asleep in your arms he was all yours, you didn't feel jealous of his own consciousness. She didn't have a jealous nature, of course, not a bit, she was only jealous of him in the sense that he had a separate being, they still had two different bloodstreams, you always hit against those ridiculous limitations. There has been no progress there at all in a million years, there was no other way to mingle except having a child together. The simplest way would be to get married, they were both strong and independent enough to put up with a certain amount of social conformity. There was no more conformity in a marriage ceremony than in a smallpox vaccination. She wasn't going to feel a bit bourgeois about it.

Toward dawn she began to feel nervous again, thinking of her father, he was an early riser, she wanted a decent time interval before facing him. He couldn't help showing a trace of tolerance, if not of irony, and it was embarrassing to face him each morning across the breakfast table, no matter how clean and fully dressed you were. And he was so careful to avoid the subject he was almost rude. Dammit, maybe it does show somehow. She did catch a couple of hours' sleep, though, so it couldn't be too bad.

– You look lovely this morning, Jess. Radiant.

– Really, you are the only man I never expected to sound cynical or cruel.

– What on earth . . .

–*Oh, ça va* . . . Your tact weighs about a ton. You make me feel I'm some sort of sex maniac, unable to talk about anything else.

– All right, then. I give up. Let's talk about it.

– Of course I've spent the night with him. Of course I'm happy. I wish I were dead.

– Yes, I know. Immortality. Make it last forever. Very tempting.

– A few more days, that's all there can be in it.

– A few days can last you a lifetime.

– Do you seriously believe in that kind of living?

– No.

– I don't think I ever knew what insecurity was, not until now. It was so safe to be in love with humanity. There are three billions of them, so you are always rich, like Albert Schweitzer. A billionaire. But when you begin to care desperately about one single human being . . .

– Are you sure you care desperately about him, Jess? Maybe you are only desperate.

– I honestly don't think I can live without him.

– Of course you can't. But you will. Life is a wonderful experience.

– Oh, please. I can almost hear the autumn leaves dropping at your feet.

– The fact is, Jessie, you make me feel so mature. . . . At the age of fifty it's quite a new thrill for me.

– But what am I to do?

– Can't you bring him here for dinner?

– I can't. You know how they feel about fathers.

– Conventional type, eh? What's he doing in Geneva, anyway?

– Waiting for the snow. A ski bum in summer.

– Sounds promising. There's nothing like stability. By the way, Jess, what's happened to the telephone? I tried to call a friend and ...

What happened to the telephone indeed. Creeping reality, that's what happened to it. It's so idiotic to go and study literature where they come and cut off your phone. She wasn't going to ask what had happened to that wonderful job of his. She had known all the time there never was a job, only rich friends. He was the sort of well-bred, distinguished-looking man to whom all sorts of sleazy parvenus liked to lend money. It's all part of buying Impressionists. He was a good status symbol, still worth a few handouts. He was still the best bait to get the Duchess of Aaren at your table, you couldn't always get the Chaplins anyway. But none of them would dream of putting him on their company's payroll: they knew where to stop. There is no such thing as a reformed alcoholic, you know. Now he was out of the bathroom, electric razor in hand, looking mildly surprised.

– There's no electricity either.

– Must be another strike. The French are always on strike, it seems.

– Jess, are we broke again?

Oh hell, let there be reality, she thought.

– Yes, we are, rather.

– How come?

– I don't know. I suppose neither of us was looking.

Let's have a moment of truth, dammit. I'm not going to baby you any longer. I'm a baby myself.

– Why didn't you tell me?

– Because we can't afford another six weeks in the clinic. We haven't finished paying them for the last. Don't look hurt. And don't tell me I remind you of my mother, because I don't feel like anybody's mother right now.

– *Oh la la!* he said. I'm afraid you *are* in love with somebody else.

She threw herself into his arms, smashing the coffeepot on her way, she was so accident-prone.

– Oh Father, Father, I don't like to play Sancho Panza to you.

– I'll fit in somehow, Jess. As I have told you, I have had an excellent business offer. . . .

– Please, please . . .

– But it's true. I was only postponing the decision a little, because I had applied for a job with the United Nations. It would have suited me perfectly. I've received a very nice letter from Adlai . . . There seems to be no opening there right now.

– So now what?

– Private enterprise, of course. Now I feel free to accept the offer I've had. Could we have some more coffee?

– They've cut off the water too. I was thinking of asking

for a grant from the Rockefeller or Ford Foundation.

– What for, Jess?

– I don't know. I seem to feel we deserve one. I don't feel it's right for them to let us become extinct. Or they could send someone to study us, I don't care. They spend millions to study and preserve all sorts of vanishing specimens. . . . Soon there'll be no one left like us. I think we should be protected and made a part of our national heritage. I'm sure they've never met anyone who is more useless, more impractical, more at odds with reality: America can really point to us with pride. I am sure the Rockefeller or the Ford Foundation would give us a grant. And then . . . they give money to poets, playwrights, painters, what's wrong with love? Why shouldn't they give it some material help before it's destroyed by environment?

– I still wish I could meet him. It's a terrible thing to have such a rival and not even know what he looks like.

– Let's try to be serious. Let's become good, useful members of society. . . .

– Please, Jess, let me do the dirty work. Anyway, as an American, there is at least one thing that gladdens my heart. We aren't typical. We are not part of the decline or fall of anything. We can go down with a clear conscience: we are marginal, irrelevant, human, in fact. The human fringe.

– Fallout. That's what some of those bums call themselves.

– Fallouts, huh. Interesting word. Expanding universe,

expanding economy, an exploding population . . . and fallouts. How true. Will you join me for lunch at the Gentilhomme? They have the best credit there.

Then two days later, as she was walking with Lenny from the boat to a café along the waterfront, Lenny grabbed her by the arm.

– Don't look—don't look, but there's a guy watching us. To the left, behind the pillar. A cop. You're not supposed to live on a boat here unless you're part of the crew. You can't live anywhere unless you're part of something. See him?

– Wait for me inside, I'll be back in a moment.

A cop indeed. He was wearing a black Homburg hat, a pin-stripe English suit, a carnation and his usual half-apologetic, half-teasing smile. Sober, thank God.

– Father, what on earth . . .

– If there must be another man in my life, I want to know what he looks like.

– Why don't you come and have a cup of coffee with us?

– No, no. Embarrassing all round.

There was a chauffeur-driven, olive-green Bentley waiting for him, the exhaust pipe puffing softly like an expensive cigar, and there was a white poodle next to the chauffeur, its head looking exactly like a chrysanthemum.

– Who is the poodle?

– My new employer. Oh, by the way, I've received an advance. Here, take this. And the poodle's secretary is

taking care of the bills. Could I have the keys to the car?
I'll need it tonight.

He kissed her on the forehead and walked wearily back
to the Bentley. It was only seven o'clock in the morning:
he must have been playing bridge all night and winning.
She wondered who the poodle was, probably one of the
Nestlé people. It's always Nestlé in Switzerland, except
when it's Sendoz. She walked to the café. There was a
plate of smoked *grison* meat on the counter and Lenny
was staring at it dreamily.

It was the meat that really did it, not him at all. He
wasn't trying anything, just feeling hungry, he had had
nothing to eat for days, so he couldn't take his eyes off the
plate, the way dogs do.

– Let's go back to the boat, Jess.

– I have to go. I have a Pushkin lecture in a half hour.

– Who's that cat?

– Pushkin was a great Russian poet.

– He sure got himself a cat's name.

– Why don't you eat that meat, Lenny, instead of staring
at it?

– What d'you mean, why? It's against the law. You've
got to pay for it, that's how mean they are.

She felt so horrified and indignant she almost burst into
tears.

– I've told you I'll do it. What are we waiting for? Why
don't you talk to your friend, instead of starving?

– Okay, okay. Don't be mad. I'll talk to him.

He grinned.

– I've made an offer. I'm not going to let you down.

– Oh, stop bragging. I know how it feels.

She decided to go to the Pushkin lecture all the same. There is no point in rejecting all spiritual help, dammit, Pushkin, Klee, the music of Boulez; one hour in the Museum of Modern Art in Basel and you feel reborn. Mankind has been seeking immortality since the beginning of time and now anyone can find it in a museum. The day Pope John XXIII died all the kids went to the Basel Museum and spent three hours looking at some of the most priceless immortality you can get outside America. In the last thirty years the American collectors have acquired more immortality and more spiritual comfort than anyone. Cornering the market.

She had to take the bus from the University, but then changed her mind and went to feed the birds by the lake, and sat there for hours with her knees drawn up under her chin. She did cry a bit at the loss of innocence, but it was only hysteria. There's absolutely nothing wrong with anything that God couldn't fix in a second and it's a truly dispiriting thought for a convinced atheist. Within a few weeks I've lost my virginity and am turning into a criminal. What next? It seems that all sorts of prospects open up for you when you are in love. I suppose when you feel the absence of God as strongly as that it's known as faith. I bet he has never heard of El Greco or Velásquez. Nothing to hold on to. You can have a perfect reproduction of Van Gogh for three Swiss francs. In the old days you had to have blind faith, but now you could see it all with your own eyes. Irony. Didn't take you very far.

It was almost 11 A.M. and she remembered it was her SPCA day and she went to the clinic and spent the rest of the day playing God to dogs, cats, monkeys and canaries. They brought you all sorts of sick and wounded pets there and it helped a little. There was particularly one red-breasted robin with a broken wing that had to be put in plaster, and she did that beautifully, and she became so absorbed in her work she was able to forget the utter wretchedness of it all and get rid of herself for a little while, it's amazing what a robin can do for you. There was nothing she hated more than sentimentality. By the end of the day she felt quite cheerful. There is nothing like playing God to make you feel human again. They had a lot of bad cases, including a six-year-old girl who brought in a dying yellow butterfly, a hopeless combination. The girl stood there crying with the butterfly in her palm, and the vet got furious, as he usually did when he felt help-less, the butterfly was still stirring a little in the child's hand, veterinary science was not yet ready to deal with such a problem, a butterfly, what next, the vet muttered. It was almost ten before she thought of going home and then remembered that her father had the car and she had to call Paul to fetch her and drive her home. The SPCA night shift was coming in, idealists who loved animals because they weren't people, lonely spinsters who simply had to give the way a cow has got to be milked, and you felt much better after a night spent attending a sick parakeet, you couldn't help feeling a little sorry for our dumb friends, everybody was asking so much of them. There was not much difference between feeling the Presence and feeling the Absence. There are moments when you feel the Absence so strongly that it becomes the Presence, you can be a good atheist and still have the problem. I suppose it all comes from being only half-cooked culturally. Even the greatest Jackson Pollock still leaves you with some secret longing. She passed on to a middle-aged lady from Lausanne, who sounded like the beginning of a limerick, the vet's instructions for one monkey with earache and the Siamese cat with gastric flu, and then Jean came to fetch her and took her for a sandwich to the *brasserie* across the street, where Paul was waiting gloomily over a glass of beer.

– What's the matter with you, Paul dear?

– Nothing. You don't love me and that's all there is to it. No wonder they have the highest suicide rate in Switzerland.

They drove her home.

It was the sweetest night of the summer, the still air was heavy with the perfumed white ghosts of orchards along the way and the reclining moon was playing Goya's *Maja Couchée* among the clouds.

They saw the Sunbeam as soon as the car turned right

from the highway into the orchard between the cherry trees, the lights jumped on it, it stood in front of the house, the engine was still running, the door was open, her father had one foot on the ground, but he hadn't quite made it, he had collapsed over the half-open door, obviously in a state of alcoholic stupor, the upper part of his body leaning over, one arm hanging limply over the door.

– Oh no, not again! Jess moaned.

– It's a long, uphill fight, Paul said, it often takes them a whole lifetime to get rid of it. The only bright side is that it gives them a purpose, something to live for.

– I'm glad I haven't paid the clinic, damn them, Jess said.

She was so furious she didn't even try to help them get him out of the car. She took one angry look at his ironic, make-believe smile, that weakling's façade, while Paul and Jean were trying to make sense of his limbs and pull him out. This was a moment when she really could have walked out on him. She left them there and went inside the house, hating practically everybody. The only good thing you could say for alcoholism was that you couldn't put it down to Western decadence, they had it in Russia too. She switched the light on, decided to hell with him, I'm not even going through the usual coffee routine, then she heard them walk in and the first sign of something wrong was the grim, strangely determined, tight expression on Jean's face. Paul's features simply didn't seem to be there any longer, only the eyes were staring at her wildly, he was trying to speak and was unable to make it, stuttering, in fact.

– J-J-Jess . . .

– What is it now? Did he drink himself dead?

– N-n-no, Paul said.

Jean grabbed her arm.

– Sit down.

– Heart attack?

– N-n-no, Paul said.

Jean pushed her toward a chair. She sat down. She knew it was the end. She knew it now. He had drunk himself dead. There is a limit to every human heart, particularly when it's truly human.

– H-h-h, Paul said.

– He has been shot, Jean said.

– Who has been shot?

– Your father has been murdered, Jean said. He's been shot in the back.

Paul was leaning against the wall, she thought give him water, she tried to rush outside, but Jean had hold of her and she tried to struggle with him, but he held her firmly.

– No, he said. No, you don't.

– What is this? she asked. What on earth is this?

– Somebody has killed your father. Sit down, Jess. Don't get hysterical, it's too easy. You'll go to pieces later, not now. Not now, Jess. Now you'll have to cope. It's serious.

– Serious?

She caught herself thinking, "It's the funniest thing," in Lenny's voice. Jean held her tight while she sobbed with laughter.

– Stop this at once, Jean said. Don't try to sneak out on it, you've got to face it now. You'll go to pieces later.

Paul had collapsed in a chair. He was trying to get up now.

– You stay there, superman, Jean told him. One is enough. Don't be cheap, Jess. Not you.

He's made it, she thought. It wasn't a relapse. It wasn't alcohol. He's made it in the end. It was the funniest thing, Lenny said, she had to laugh. She felt Jean's slap burning her face.

– I don't need the routine, Jean. I'm all right.

– Sit down here.

– I'm all right, damn you, she said.

– P-p-please.

She shouldn't have said that. It only made him stutter again. She had to laugh. It was the funniest thing.

She went hysterical again and Jean stopped stuttering. Now Paul was here too and she drank it all while he was holding a glass to her lips, then she realized suddenly it was not like a nightmare at all, it was much worse, it looked like reality and she went off again, but when she came around Paul was holding her hands while Jean was going through the living room throwing things on the floor, smashing a lamp, throwing books around, opening drawers and breaking the window glass. This time it did look like some nightmare, but then Jean came back and leaned over her.

– Can you make sense now, Jess?

– What's all this? For God's sake, what is all this?

– We've got to call the police, so you'd better try to make it look right.

Make it look right. She was sure she had heard him say that.

– Stop it, Jess, or I'll really have to beat you up, Jean said. I mean it. Listen. You will have to make sense. Look at that.

He was taking something from his pocket and showing it to her. Gold coins.

– I found them all over the car, Jean said. Hundreds of them. Your father was smuggling gold into Switzerland and somebody got him. Do you hear me? Your father was smuggling gold.

She was staring at the gold coins in his hand. Export-import. I've come to a sudden conclusion, Jess. What conclusion? Humility. I'm going to become stinking rich. Who am I to refuse to stink? I'll fit in somehow. The nature of reality. Money. We are going to conform. A villa in the South of France. Picassos. No more escapism. Hard-boiled materialism. You can't lick them, join them. I'm going to make money. There must be something about it. Some hidden charm. Let's try money, Jess. We've never tried money, have we?

She was beginning to smile again.

– No, you don't, Jean said.

– I'm all right, she said.

I suspect it's all Samson Delila and his Pussycats.

– Please don't cry, Jess.

– It's the funniest thing, she said.

– Jess.

– I was the one who was supposed to do that. I was going to do that for him. He did that for me . . . Oh God.

Oh God. You say that, but you know it's only Samson Delila and his Pussycats.

– We have to call the police, so please try to make sense.

Sense? Yes, I suppose that's another name for it. It all makes sense. He didn't give me time, I was going to do it.

– Here, take my hand.

– I'm all right. It's the funniest thing, really. . . .

The funniest thing. And it was then that it hit her. It was then that it came back to her. Lenny. *They've found somebody else*. Who? I don't know. *Plenty of good will around*. She sat very stiff, very still in her chair. Lenny. They've found somebody else all right.

– Kids, do you have a gun? Can one of you give me a gun?

– Stop that cheap crap, none of that cut wrist nonsense, Jean said.

They had found somebody else, they had been playing on both of them separately, on her father and her, and he knew that all the time, plenty of good will around, the bastard. I'm not going to cry as long as I live and he's going to pay for it. There's going to be one more dead rat in this world.

– Jess, you've got to listen.

– I'm listening, damn you.

– We're going to tell the police there has been a robbery here, your father came back, found them and they killed him. We're going to make it look right. Open doors, disorder, smashed things, all that. They killed him in panic, okay?

– Okay.

– You've got to keep your head. You don't want them to find out that your father was smuggling gold, you don't want that.

– Yes, it's bad for American prestige, isn't it?

– He's dead, so you might try to make it look clean, you can do that for him. Do you hear what I'm saying, *nom de Dieu?*

The rat. The clever, cynical little rat. I'll do all I can, I'll find a way. I'll hurt him so he'll never get over it. Never. I'll show him there's plenty of good will around.

– I don't know if you're going to make it, but you're going to try. I'm going to call them now.

They came. The moment she saw them, the feeling of reality became so strong and final that she ran out into the garden and was sick. They moved around in a heavy, matter-of-fact way, it was all routine to them and their feet were all over the place like some kind of scavenging, crawling rodents who feed on reality. She remained sitting in a chair, her nails sunk deep into the leather, trying not to scream while they were asking questions. The two boys stood by her, telling them angrily to leave her alone but there was no one else to turn to, it was all only crumbling Mayan temples and carefully preserved picturesque cathedrals. And there was no one bigger to hate than a rat.

– Are you sure there is nothing of value missing?

Nothing of value missing. It was the funniest thing, she had to laugh.

– They don't seem to have taken anything.

– It depends on the sense of values you have, Inspector, Paul said.

She looked up at them. She felt all right now. There weren't going to be any more hysterics.

– I have a diplomatic passport. My father and I are covered by diplomatic immunity. Nothing can happen to us. Nothing can touch us.

– Jess. Jess.

– You know about diplomatic immunity, Inspector? It gives you total protection.

– Jess.

She almost went to the kitchen to make him some strong coffee, it will sober him up, but shook it off instantly, no more of that, no more dramatics, no cheap, easy way out, you're going to face it, it's only life, she even went upstairs to give them a sheet to cover the body, but didn't go outside to look at it for the last time, when they carried it to the ambulance, you have to know your limits. They had put a blanket on her knees and thrown a coat over her shoulders. She stayed on the chair shivering a little and Jean was sitting on the floor beside the chair, holding her hand, Paul was pressing a cup of coffee to her lips, you can't go wrong with coffee, you have always got coffee to fall back on, except in the underdeveloped countries, where they've still got religious mania. What can I do to get religious mania back, somehow? How do you become an American primitive again? How do you crawl back to Grandma Moses? You can't, you've gone too Stanislavski about it all, realism. He was a lovely human being who happened to be also a Pope, Cardinal Montini, looking like a clever Jewish lawyer from New York, it's only pop art really. Living is like beating your wings against an invisible window pane, who wrote that? It's all so absurd there must be a Nobel Prize for literature in it. All the lights were blazing in the house and she could hear the birds singing in the orchard, the lights woke them up and they thought it was dawn, while they carried her to the ambulance, half unconscious with dope, and then she woke up in some clinic, white walls, white nuns, a Catholic setup, obviously, with a crucifix on the wall, and she wished angrily that she had taken with her her reproduction of Marcel Duchamp's *Nu Descendant l'Escalier* to take its place, for spiritual comfort, and in case she felt like believing in something that was truly there.

They kept her more or less continuously doped during

the first two or three days and then they made her get up and made her walk around, her mind blank, emptied by sleep, which is known as feeling better. Then the pain and the anguish returned and so they pronounced her cured. She stayed in her room, staring ahead with an empty gaze and only tears came to fill the void. The kids were there every morning, but she refused to see them. She didn't want anything human around her. There was a thirst in her, an angry, impetuous craving that none of the miracle pills the nuns gave her were able to calm. The pills were called *benzyl-methyl-isoxazolylcarbonyl-hydrazene,* it sounded like the names of some Aztec gods, the nuns were very *à la page.* She rested in the garden in a wicker chair, her shoulders wrapped in a shawl, with a book of Klee's reproductions on her lap, and whenever the longing became more than she could bear, she leafed through the pages slowly: Klee alone never failed her. The magical power of his hand gave to the so-called real world the ephemeral quality of a passing shadow. Grace was the only word that could describe this wonder. Or you could call it God, for the lack of a better term, the way each funny, human face, a bug, a bird, was touched with a light of loveliness and gaiety. She had always believed in Klee, but never more fervently than now. In fact, she had tears in her eyes, looking at the reproduction of his "Blue Pebbles with Bird." You always feel closer to some artist than to others, not unlike in medieval times, when everybody used to have a favorite saint and put himself under his protection. People had all sorts of so-called mystical experiences, contemplating the ocean or the Grand Canyon, but Klee didn't need so much space, he made you feel his living presence on a sheet of paper sixteen inches by twelve. Nature was a magnificent accident, a confrontation of matter, time and chance, but behind the beauty of Klee you knew the presence of a guiding hand, a purpose, the warm glow of love, the pervading mastery of mind and will. There was almost no limit to what great art could do for you. There was a tremendous work to be done, a kind of cultural evangelism, most of the world still lives in a materialistic wilderness, it is simply heartbreaking to think that there is Klee when millions of people in dire need of spiritual help do not even know his name.

Next morning when she woke up, R.F. walked in, looking unfinished without his pipe. She smiled: he will have to go back to his artist for one more sitting.

– *Ça va mieux?* Good. Here is a little present for you.

It was a book of reproductions of the frescoes Matisse did for a chapel in the South of France. She didn't care for Matisse, too French, too lucid, no mystery. He seemed content with the earth and to have never felt a craving, a thirst for some superior, transcendental beauty. French painting remained essentially terrestrial. The only transcendental art comes from America today, abstract expressionism was pure metaphysics, they were truly challenging religion on its own ground. You could call them metaphysical atheists, really; they did succeed in bringing you a lot nearer to some hidden truth. Even the new pop art was better, a mesmerized, self-hating coming to grips with environment and materialism, it had an authentic quality of despair in it. But the only artist who could help her now was Klee, you couldn't call him a religious or a mystical painter, in any way, thank God, but he did convey to you a hint of a universal smile around you, in which all things nestled. It was nothing but poetry, of course. She still felt a bit sur-realistic from sedatives, but she did manage to talk to R.F. rather coherently, she thought, and he was nodding all the time, so she was obviously making sense. Yes, he told her, he knew exactly what she was trying to say, there were a lot of kids today, particularly American, who seemed thirst-drunk, if he could put it that way, his English wasn't too good. The thirst-drunk generation, he called them. He was probably referring to their thirst for culture. They found themselves in full agreement there. Actually, there was little doubt, in her opinion, that art was on the verge of some tremendous discovery. It was poised for a fantastic leap into the unknown and no one could tell what miracles it was going to perform. It was heading in that direction. The earth will be covered with fabulous museums and you won't even have to go there, it will all come to you. Whenever you feel what is commonly known, to use a convenient cliché, as "the deep craving of the human soul," it will all come to you through the miracle of electronics, you will press a button and suddenly, out of the darkness, out of nothing-ness, the greatest of all Kandinskys will come to life before you. Oh God, it will be absolutely marvelous. She sobbed and sobbed, and R.F. held her hand and the nuns were scuttling around like white mice and then gave her some pills again. She lay waiting for the stuff to work, her eyes wide open, almost peaceful now, her heart filled with certitude at last. A fantastic cultural renaissance, an artistic awakening of a fabulous magnitude. She went on discussing it with R.F. for a while, perhaps a little confusedly now, and they found themselves in full agreement once more, great art had unlimited spiritual perspectives. The Dominican was not a narrow-minded religious bigot and she certainly wasn't a narrow-minded atheist, either. She felt much comforted before she passed out, after they agreed to go and look at the Klee exhibition next week.

Then her mind cleared and everything was bitterness again. Her first tribute to lucidity was to ask how much the clinic cost, just to get the feel of things again. She was told that Paul was taking care of that. So it was charity now. She decided to stay another day or two and then volunteer for the Peace Corps. The Peace Corps was a kind of Foreign Legion a girl could join to get rid of herself. And then it's quite remarkable what fascination the word *peace* could have for you, given the proper circumstances. She quite successfully avoided thinking of her father, it only made her think of that rat again. Her SPCA days were over. Hard as nails. Getting rid of all the lyrical puppy fat at last. With a little luck she could still make it and become the toughest bitch around. Fitting in, there's something to be said for conformity. She even went as far as painting her toenails bright red in front of the nuns, just to tell them where they got off. Humming a tune. Listening to jazz records. Smoking a cigarillo, standing naked in front of a mirror, looking at her body, she might still need that. Becoming a top-class call girl, just for reality. You can say it all with contraceptives. She had exactly the right kind of body for aggressive self-expression. You can get rid of almost anything in a striptease joint, yourself included. Promiscuity should help, too. But there was no way of punishing her father now, as far as that was concerned, Lenny was all she had left. But there was no way of reaching him, not even by becoming a whore. It can only hurt somebody who cares. That's what loneliness really means: loneliness, it's when you can't hurt anybody. All you can do then is to try to punish yourself. Then a sudden surge of blind, dumb, animal anguish would sweep away every painfully assumed attitude, tear to bits every shred of composure, of courage, and there would be nothing left of her but shaking shoulders, the cold indifference of the wet pillow against her face, and the only self-fulfillment that always seems open to you, the infuriating, humiliating self-fulfillment of tears.

It would take her hours then before she could even attempt to reach for irony again.

The kids came back and tried the H-bomb on her, but it didn't help. Chuck brought her a copy of James Baldwin's *The Fire Next Time,* but she didn't find it satisfactory, it's always next time with them. But she wasn't going to do like

Marilyn Monroe, either. There must be some ways of expressing yourself other than pills, booze or promiscuity.

Money.

It came so suddenly and so quietly, she didn't even realize it was there at first. It's always like that with true inspiration.

She smiled, lit a cigarillo and lay very still, looking through the open window at the empty sky.

The inspiration was there, all right, in the quiet hatred of her heart. She truly felt the presence of the muse, as they used to say in the old romantic days.

Money. It was such a perfect medium for self-expression. You'll have to use it the way Jackson Pollock used paint. Splashing it all over the empty canvas in long, bold strokes. After all, that's what materialism is all about: splashing money all over the empty canvas, trying to fill it with something.

Swimming pools. Minks. Rolls-Royces. Villas everywhere. Jewels. Clothes. The ultimate in pop art. Money, reality at its lousiest best. And there would be no uphill fight for recognition, everybody understands money, you don't need an education. It has a universal appeal, exactly what all great art should have. There must have been other artists who had thought of that medium before, but they couldn't lay their hands on it. She could. *A Quality of Despair*. A title was not enough. Now she had something to go with it. She had something to say at last.

She could almost see the bank manager's face, an open,

receptive face. You could put anything in there, you knew it would bring an income.

"I would like to open a bank account."

"Yes, Miss Donahue. By all means. How much do you wish to deposit?"

"I don't really know yet. Two, three hundred thousand dollars? Is that all right?"

"It's perfectly all right, Miss Donahue. You don't have to be rich to open a bank account in Switzerland."

She smiled. She was beginning to enjoy her money already. She lit another cigarillo and lay in her bed very quietly, smiling, imagining it all, putting a nice little artistic touch here and there for realism.

"Would you wish us to invest it for you?"

"No, I would like you to set up a trust for dumb animals."

"What kind of dumb animals do you have in mind, Miss Donahue?"

"Oh, stray dogs. Rats. Birds."

"We could still invest it for you. Then the animals would get the income without touching the capital."

"No, I don't wish to invest it. I don't want them to get rich. They might become human."

That was a rather good, cruel, punishing stroke, she thought. It was all taking shape in her mind quite clearly now. It was very dangerous, of course, it was probably going to kill her, but that had always been the fate of the artist breaking new ground.

"Please draw up the papers immediately. I'm rather in a hurry. You see, I'm going to die. It's the heart. I've probably got only a few days to live."

"I'm terribly sorry to hear this, Miss Donahue. Terribly sorry."

"Oh, that's quite all right. I don't mind a bit. Only, please see to it all at once. And don't forget the birds. I want a million dollars or so to go to the birds."

"Any specific birds, Miss Donahue?"

"Seagulls. All migratory birds. All kinds."

"You have to be quite specific about that, in order to avoid litigation. Are there any you wish to be excluded?"

"Only vultures and the like."

"I see. Birds of prey to be excluded."

She was puffing on her cigarillo, enjoying herself.

And then massive gold bathroom fixtures, of course. It's got to be massive, it always is. Rubies, emeralds and the like. The fastest Italian cars.

– Kids, do you know about pop? It's the latest back home. I'm thinking of going into that in a big way.

They eyed her rather suspiciously. They probably thought she was still a bit dopy. Paul had been pacing the floor, talking of sainthood, how he was going to dedicate his life to nothing and become a modern saint. It is strange how nothing is on everybody's mind in Switzerland. Too much of everything, I suppose. Now he was observing her with a cold, Olympian calm, an expression of perfect self-control he always assumed when he was about to explode.

– W-w-w? Jean remarked.

He was okay now, back to normal. He was wearing a red polo shirt and a red blazer, in the hope of distracting your attention from the tender vulnerability written all over his face. He had brought her an enormous bouquet of lilacs and had settled in a chair for the day, with a book of poetry. Ronsard, too. After a couple of hours he had raised his blue eyes from the book and told her earnestly, and a bit sadly:

– Y-you know, J-Jess, whenever I r-read poetry, it always s-seems as if it had been written about y-y-you.

Sweet.

Now he had closed his book and seemed worried. Paul dug his hands deep into his pockets, expressing himself only with his angry elbows.

– What are you talking about?

– Oh, come on. Pop art. Surely you've heard about that. It's going very strong right now back in the States. It's the ultimate in American culture, in fact. They use junk for creative self-expression. Beer cans, bottles, streetcars, packs of cigarettes, all kinds of trash. They're filling all the art galleries in New York with it. Coming to terms with the environment, I suppose.

– Of course I know about pop, pussycat. Dollar bills, jukeboxes, frigidaires, garbage, painted with love, servility, acceptance and dedication. They have quite a big spiritual revival in your country.

– Well, what about it?

– What about what?

– I feel like starting a collection. De-luxe pop. Minks. Diamonds. Balenciaga. Bullfights in Spain. The Ritz everywhere.

– What are you going to do for money, love?

She told them. They looked at her silently for a while. Then Jean picked up his book again.

– You're only after him again, that's all, Paul told her, his voice quivering with anger.

– Nonsense.

– Oh, come on. You're only out to get that son of a bitch. You're still in love with him, or you wouldn't be hating him so much.

– Stop being so damn French about it.

She looked at Jean.

– P-Paul is right. *C-crime p-passionel,* that's what you have in mind, Jess.

She glared at them. She had all her strength back now, there is nothing like suddenly finding a purpose in life again.

– Listen, you two, my father got killed because he wanted to make me rich. All right, I'm going to fulfill his dream. I'm going to make myself rich. It's the least I can do for him. An act of love. I suppose neither of you knows what that is.

Her voice shook a little. That did it. Jean came over and took her hand and Paul turned white with rage. It was in the bag.

– All right, then. This is going to be a students' prank to end all students' pranks, including probably these three students as well.

– You don't have to do it.

– Stop being so damn coy, Jess. Whom are you trying to kid? You don't care a damn about the money. It's all strictly between you and him. You're still in love with that bum, so it's pure hate now. I'm sick of both of you. I've had about all I can take from love. Why can't you build a nice home together instead of destroying each other? Same thing. Or why can't you marry Jean, if you really feel suicidal. You'll only appreciate me better. What are you going to do with the *fric*?

– I told you. Wallow in it.

– Ah, come off it. You couldn't care less about money. Just a bloody excuse.

– All right, then, we could give it to the hospitals, to the aged. . . . Or even better, to the Ban-the-Bomb fund.

– Ha ha, that's exactly what I thought. Jean, this girl is the vanishing American idealist. I have read about them in history books. No, sweetie, I'll come along with your nice little scheme, but only if you let me throw that filth, once we get hold of it, where it belongs: down the sewer.

– Paul, honestly, you can't do that. There are people starving everywhere.

Paul stopped pacing the floor and stared at her with utmost scorn. Elbows again. Neurotic.

– You know something? You're cheap.

– Oh, shut up, P-P-Paul. We can find a dozen other f-fellows to help us. The G-G-Gennaro twins.

She gave up. There was no use pretending any longer.

– I don't care a damn what you are going to do with the money, Paul. Not a damn.

– That's better. It's exactly what I thought. Okay, I'll come along. I hope somebody gets killed, preferably him. Russian roulette. I've had enough of the four of us. So the Puritan Army is on the move again. General Calvin will be pleased to hear that. I may even put on my army uniform for the occasion. After all, it's a highly patriotic task we're going to perform. Freeing Switzerland from materialistic garbage. This country has been occupied by money long enough. Let's get rid of some of it at least. We'll fight it on the hills and in the fields, we'll fight it in the banks and on the beaches, we'll never surrender. . . .

– I-i-it's going to be our p-proudest hour.

– Right, let's hit the jungle trail. The safari is on. Big-game hunting in Geneva again.

She smiled. It was the funniest thing. Big-game hunting is quite a name when you are only out to get a rat.

14

HE WAITED FOR HER A WHOLE WEEK. HE HADN'T LEFT
the boat all this time, so he knew she didn't show up. Probably found another guy. That's how it always ends with sex.
He didn't care a damn, he could drop dead right now as
far as he was concerned, that's how little it all meant to
him. Then he went to the SPCA looking for her and they
told him to take his turn and he sat for hours between a
chimpanzee with an arm in a sling and a pekingese who
had worms. She didn't show up and he went back to the
boat and gave her another chance. He didn't eat or sleep,
that's how fed up with her he was. You could have too
much of a good thing. Or maybe she's got demography,
not taking care of herself, and didn't want to tell him.
Silly bitch. What do I care if she's got herself pregnant?
The way I feel about marriage, I could marry her tomorrow, it means nothing to me. It can't hurt you, as long as
it's all the same to you. But it was no good. He sat on his
berth in the dark, his face in his hands. He could almost
feel life turning important on him. So what? You can
make too much of nothing. If you believe in nothing too

much, this is known as principles. If you fight life propaganda all the time, this is known as dedication. I'm no shit hero. I don't stick to principles. I don't care a damn if I get married to her and have five kids and go back home and get a job, it's all the same to me. It's all such a joke anyway, I might as well raise a family and get a really good laugh out of it. She's probably going to have an abortion and she's scared to tell me. It was true that he liked kids a lot and he didn't want to have any of his own, he was against cruelty. You can't help being born yourself, but you don't have to do that to others. Still, if she got herself pregnant he didn't care. Let the kid be born and live, the hell with principles. I'm sick and tired of trying to make sense. Then he shook his head till his blond hair was all over his face and grinned. Jesus, he thought. Am I meditating? What next?

In the end it hit him so hard he went to see the Negro broad just for company. He had to wait outside her room until she finished with a customer. He opened the window for fresh air, then sat on the bed scowling at her.

– How many guys do you have in a night?

– Why, sonny? You want a cut?

– Why don't you go back home, stupid?

– No sir. Not as long as they've got segregation there.

Principles, he thought. She's got principles, that kid.

He looked at her bare buttocks while she was putting on fresh lipstick, and at her breasts. She had huge, round, bulging mass media, no question about that.

– Here in Europe you feel you're the same as anyone
else, she said. You can keep your self-respect.

– Where do you keep it?

She caught his eye.

– Not there, sonny. That's got nothing to do with it.

Crazy. She was walking around, naked, teasing him
back and front. He grabbed her gown and threw it at
her.

– Put that over your mass media, honey, I'm feeling
cold.

– You still in love, sonny?

– Where's Angel?

– Around. I don't like that guy. Real mean. He don't
even let you take off your clothes. He's always after your
self-respect. You still in love with that chick, sonny?

– I'm still working on her, if that's what you mean.

She picked up the *Herald Tribune* from under a chair.

– You saw that?

Former U.S. Diplomat Murdered in Gen . . .

Jesus Christ. He went quite numb for a moment, then
he felt his diaphragm in his throat again.

– Jesus Christ, he said.

– Yeah, I guess you can say that. Some thieves. All they
took was a pair of cufflinks and a watch. You saw this item
here? That's why I saved the paper. They're using electric
prods on civil rights folks in Mississippi. Like they were
cattle.

He grabbed the *Trib* and ran back to the boat and

waited. He felt much better now. She didn't turn up because she had motivation, the best excuse he could think of. Now she'd come, he knew that. She needed him now. He read and reread the piece in the paper a hundred times. A pair of gold cufflinks and a watch. Killing a man for that. Jesus Christ.

It was 5 A.M. He could hear the first gulls waking up on the water, then there were footsteps on the deck and he jumped up from the berth and saw her come down. He knew at once something was wrong. Not her father, something personal. She looked at him like he was there no more. He had started to say gee, Jess, I'm sorry, but she caught him smack on the mouth with that wild, not-here look in her eyes and he knew it was something personal, it had to be.

Through Mount Palomar, that's how she kept staring at him. The greatest telescope in the world. He felt a million light-years away and it made him feel good all of a sudden, it made him feel himself again, like he was no longer there at all, and there's just nothing better than that, what more can you ask?

Only, Jesus, why pick on me like that? What have I done?

Then she saw the *Trib* on the floor. *Former U.S. Diplomat Murdered in Gen* . . .

– How does it feel to read about yourself in the papers, Lenny?

He didn't get that one at first.

– Gee, Jess, I'm sorry. They found out who's done it?

– No, you don't have to worry yet.

– What you talking about?

– Oh, come off it. You know what I'm talking about. My father was smuggling gold into Switzerland. Your friends killed him. Or maybe you did.

He went blank for a couple of years. Nothing. Then he heard the gulls again, a piercing, bloody shriek, right from the diaphragm.

– The paper says it was a robbery.

She shrugged.

– Did you do it, Lenny? Did you have anything to do with it? As a matter of curiosity?

It was the worst blow that had ever hit him, although some of them he couldn't remember, so there's no telling. But it hit him so hard all he could think of was how to hide the hurt. Pride. He didn't know he still carried that around.

– Why, Jess, if I had killed your father I'd have told you so right away. It's always the first thing I tell a girl.

She nodded approvingly, like she knew it all. Like she had a lifetime of information. You kept forgetting she was only a kid.

– That's right, Lenny. That's the spirit. Real cool. Let's play some more. I don't mind if you killed my father, as long as you love me. The world is a sick joke, isn't that right? Look, Ma, no hands, the thalidomide kid said. That's the mentality, isn't it? You see, I'm catching up fast.

Amoral. Free. Existentialist. I bet you don't even know you're that. Anti-crap. Anti-corn. Anti-propaganda. That's how full of crap, that's how full of corn, that's how full of propaganda you are.

He didn't get that one. Advanced Studies at Princeton, that must be it. That was something Bug Moran was always talking about. Advanced Studies at Princeton thought-shit. She was going psychological on him.

– Jess, I wouldn't kill a man even if they paid me. I'm not that big. I haven't got it in me. Not yet. Maybe someday. You've got to have maturity to do a thing like that.

He hated that cold look in her eyes. Cruelty to animals, that's what it was. Then she'll go and work at the SPCA some more.

– I don't know a thing about it. You sure built me up big in your dreams. Real big. Think, kid. Why the hell would I keep after you if I already knew they had your father working for them?

– That's why you kept after me, of course.

– Sure, sure, that's why, in the beginning. Only in the beginning. Then I got hung up on you. I got hung up on you real bad. I still am.

Jesus, he thought. I shouldn't be saying this. She'll never believe me. I'm telling only the God's truth, so how can she believe me? If only I could find a good lie, something that would really make sense here. But he couldn't. He didn't feel a bit like lying, that's how low he felt.

– I guess they had me working on you while they were

working on your old man. I guess they didn't think I had
it in me. I told them you'd do it for me.

– You were so damn sure of it?

– Yeah, I was sure. I was so hung up on you I started
to believe in myself again. You gave me my overconfidence
back. I was sure.

– You were right. Why, then? Why did they go to him?

– Maybe they got impatient. You were slow to come
along, Jess. Very slow.

– Are you trying to tell me it's my fault that my father
is dead?

– No, no. I don't say that. Can't you see I'm all shook
up? I'm only trying to figure, that's all.

It could be Angel all right. Or could be somebody else.
Some other crowd. Plenty of good will around.

But she had made up her mind, he could see that. It
had to be him. She liked the idea.

Jesus Christ, the way those gulls are screaming you'd
think it hurts them too.

Just because I've laid you, kid, that doesn't figure I'm
a murderer.

I couldn't even kill myself, so why should I go and do
a favor to a guy I've never met?

He shook his head.

– Crazy, your old man doing this for you, while you
were doing it for him. Didn't you two ever talk to each
other?

He didn't mean it that way, but she looked like she was

going to cry, and then what do you know, she slapped him, smack across his big mouth. . . . But he didn't mind. He grinned. At least they were in touch again.

– Are you trying to tell me it's all over between us, Jess? Something like that? Because I feel for me life is just beginning.

He meant it, too. He felt like life was just beginning, that's how goddamn awful he felt.

– Well, kid, I'm glad you dropped in to say hello.

– Shut up. Listen, now. You'll go see Angel. You'll tell him I'll go through with it now. I'm ready to take the stuff across the frontier any time. Today, tomorrow. Any time.

He just sat there, gaping. It made no sense at all. So she probably meant it.

– Jesus, he said. What makes you want to do it now? And I mean *now*?

– They killed my father, didn't they?

– What kind of sense is that? You aren't trying to play cops and robbers, Jess? They'll kill you. They'd kill both of us.

She almost smiled.

– That would really be a fate worse than death, Lenny. Being stuck with you for eternity.

– I'm not joking. They'd kill you.

– So what? What's so great about life, Lenny, all of a sudden?

I'm going to give it to her. She's asking for it.

– You really want to know?

– Yes, from the horse's mouth. Tell me. What's so great about life, Lenny?

He took his time.

– You.

That really threw her. For one moment he even thought he was going to fall for it himself, that's how good he was. He had the best face around for sincerity, all the bums told him that. You have the best shit face for heartbreak, Lenny, they kept repeating. You can't miss. You'll always make a living, even when there's no snow around. You're the kind of bum who'll always scrape through the summer months as long as broads have maternity down there. You have just the right kind of looks, you lucky bastard. He was so good at lying and it came so true and natural and honest he almost fell for it himself. His throat was tight and he could feel his diaphragm kicking and jumping, or whatever they put in there when they bring you down here for a visit. I'm just too good at it. Or maybe you can't trust a lie any more, it goes true on you all of a sudden. I guess it gets you subliminal, all the life propaganda. That's always the way mass media work.

– Anything you say, kid. I'll go and talk to Angel. I better make sense, though. Why is it so important to you all of a sudden? Money, I mean. What's your motivation? Because you've got motivation, I can see that.

– Lenny, my father got himself killed because he wanted me to be rich. I'm going to be as rich as he tried to make me. You didn't know my father. You didn't know how he cared about money. That's the one thing he believed in. He was a hard-boiled, practical realist. Only Cadillacs. That's why my mother left him: because he was too materialistic. He wanted me to be rich, I'm going to do that for him. That's known as filial piety. Okay?

Irony. I better watch my ass. She's got motivation all right.

– Okay. Makes sense. I'll go see Angel right away. You sure begin to measure up, kid.

He reached for his shirt and started to put it on. With his head half hidden under the shirt, he stopped dead and sat still a moment. He simply didn't have the strength to make a move.

– I had nothing to do with it, Jess. You must believe me.

– That would take a lot of proving.

– How d'you want me to prove it? Just how?

– Go and tell Angel I'll take the gold in for him.

– What the hell will that prove? Suppose he says no?

– He'll only say no if you warn him. The police think it was a robbery. I'm supposed to think that too. I found out by accident, because there were gold coins all over the car. Angel doesn't know that. Nobody does. Tell him I'm alone, broke and desperate, and that I'll do anything for dough right now. Tell him. It makes sense.

It did, too. She's after my ass, that's what it is. She thinks I had something to do with it and she's out to get me.

– Suppose he says no all the same? What then?

– I can't think that far. I hear a top-class call girl can make over a hundred dollars a day in Geneva, easy.

Baby talk, he thought. He felt like grabbing her and running away somewhere simple. Real far. Outer Mongolia. What was that place in Asia, like Outer Mongolia, only farther away? Euthanasia, that was it.

With his head and face still hidden under his shirt and only his blond hair showing, he said:

– Euthanasia, that's where I feel like going right now. I don't know where it is, but it sounds far enough to me.

It was only ages-old maternal instinct, but she felt a blind, almost animal urge to take him in her arms. For one brief moment it was again like something that had fallen out of a nest. It was like look what happened to Huckleberry Finn again. He was good at it. Damn good.

– Stop working on me, Lenny. There's no point now.

He pulled his shirt down, looking pained.

– Why do you say that?

– Okay, okay, hurry up. I'll be waiting at eleven at the Louis d'Or bar. Call me there, yes or no.

– Jess, listen to me. . . .

She shrugged angrily, the way the French do, and turned her back on him, and he hated to let her go like that. He hated to let her go.

Jesus.

He tried to find something to say to himself, he was beginning to feel sorry for the bastard.

There must be a Chinese cookie for it.

Some kind of sukiyaki or matchupitchu or whatever those oriental pearls of detachment are called. But he couldn't think of one right now.

He still hurt all over from the overkill. Dazed, sort of.

I've got to go and see Angel and tell him. As soon as I get my breath back.

I'll bet she'll turn me in to the police at the frontier, so I'll be rid of her. She's so full of motivation she's burning with it.

He could see through the porthole Geneva coming up for daylight, with the Movado, Omega, Fly Swissair and Nestlé signs glowing bright and hopeful against the sky.

They must be the best-fed seagulls around here and still crying out for something extra. Human, kind of.

She made you think of something they have in the movies, wide screen. The way she was burning with it.

He tried to remember what it was. Christians, that's the word. First Christians. Lions. Martyrs. Ben-Hur. Jesus Christ, Cinerama.

She had no business to look at a human being like that. It was cruelty to animals.

I must go and see Angel right away, yes or no.

He sat still on the berth in the first light of dawn, holding his face in his hands. It must weigh about a hundred pounds, he thought. I didn't know you could have that much on your diaphragm. It must be the heaviest diaphragm in the world.

Jesus, I wish I had maturity, like guys who go and hang themselves.

15

THERE WAS A NEW SCHOOL OF TRANSCENDENTAL AB-
straction in Paris; its adepts stood in front of an empty
canvas with an imaginary brush in their hand, going
through a pantomime of the act of painting, thus expressing
their absolute rejection of all compromise with being and
matter, including that of art itself, and one of their works
had been bought for fifteen thousand dollars by the
Twentieth Century Museum in Geneva, a perfect illu-
stration of Malraux's *Voices of Silence*. She spent an hour
or so looking at it, and the statement was quite convincing,
life and art were truly one in the empty frame, it was
like getting somewhere at last, and it was as far as you
could go without retreating into some religion or other.
Chuck stood by her side, nervously steadying his glasses,
watching the blankness with a kind of scared incredu-
lity.

– That's too far out for me, Jess. It's too figurative,
that's what I mean. Too realistic in its representation of
nothing. I don't dig realism, I guess.

There was a room of new Americans in the museum
and she had never felt closer to the young rebellious pop
artists obsessed by the materialistic garbage around them,

painting a can of Heinz soup with a kind of pure, fascinated hate. In a way it was an almost metaphysical experience. There was no doubt that if you stood long enough in front of a painting representing a can of Heinz soup you couldn't help sensing the presence of another, different and bigger truth. It was the funniest thing. She had to laugh.

– What's the matter with you, Jess? You're so damn sarcastic.

– I found myself, Chuck.

– What's that supposed to mean?

– I've finally found a medium in which I can express myself. It's not going to be literature or painting.

– Sex?

– No, Chuck. Money.

– Well, that's a good medium, if you can lay your hands on it. So you've found yourself, eh? I bet that means you're still lost, only more so.

– Chuck, how'd you like to earn the fifty francs I still owe you?

At 11 A.M. she sat at the bar of the Louis d'Or, eating olives and waiting for Lenny's call. There was no one she knew there, except one of her father's drinking friends, who came over and held her hand, looking at her tearfully. Almost all the drunks she had ever known had blue eyes.

– Such a terrible thing, my dear. He was a wonderful man. I have a feeling of a cruel personal loss.

She glanced at his martini.

– Yes, I suppose you feel as if my father had joined Alcoholics Anonymous.

The man was shocked. So cynical, *n'est-ce pas?* The young people today are so hostile and heartless. She felt in the right mood.

Then Lenny called, it was okay, same day, 2 P.M., four miles off the frontier, French side, there was a little field there behind the ruin of a barn with a faded Cinzano sign on the wall. She phoned Paul immediately at the Red Button headquarters and was told that the Gennaro twins were in on it now and so was almost everybody else there, the whole Puritan Army was mad with excitement and eager to go. She had a few more olives and a canapé. She was feeling exactly like Eisenhower on D-Day, except that it wasn't raining.

At 2 P.M. she sat in her Sunbeam in the field, under the Cinzano sign. It was a beautiful day. One of those days you shouldn't be trying to do something about it, really. With a bit of cheap romanticism you could even read a sort of loving and compassionate smile into the tenderness of light and air. I'm getting lyrical again, must be nerves. She put Handel's *Messiah* on the record player, and those heavenly choirs seemed like the right kind of welcome for a lot of dough. Then she saw in her mirror a black Buick drive into the field and her heart jumped a bit faster, but it was only because she saw Lenny. Hate at first sight, as usual. There was another young man with him, sitting behind the wheel, white-faced, sharp-featured, mean, obviously real, and for one brief second the heavenly choirs of Handel's *Messiah* seemed a bit panicky. She took her lipstick from her purse and began to paint her lips carefully, looking at herself in the mirror, it somehow seemed the right, cool thing to do. Then Lenny came up to her and she handed him the key, still busy with her lipstick. Though why the hell I should feel scared with my life behind me anyway, I don't know. She watched them in the mirror while they were busy taking a suitcase out of the back of the Buick, then into the luggage compartment of the Sunbeam. Lenny jumped in beside her and handed her the key.

– Okay, let's go.

She drove the car out of the field and onto the road. His blond hair was all over the place, it was better not to look. It's what's known as a good physique, that's all. She saw the black Buick hovering behind them for a while, but it had to go through the papers and customs check and that ought to give them just about enough time.

– Where do I get my twelve thousand?

– Geneva.

He was watching her, but you couldn't tell. It was a tossup. He did feel his throat a little tight with suspense. I've got curiosity, that's all. She needed the money real bad, true enough, but then Angel had warned him there was a twenty percent reward on any gold catch by the customs, so she was sure to collect, regardless. So it had to be personal. All I know is that she has it for me one way or the other, or she wouldn't be driving so desperate. Hundred and ten, hundred and twenty. Jesus, that's one way of still making it together. Hundred and thirty, almost. Fancy hating poor Lenny's guts like that, this is pure love or else I don't know what pure love is. Murder. Trees flying over your head. You felt no earth under you any longer. She's still stuck on me, so I guess she's warned the police. She gives it a last chance, though. Tears in her eyes, looking tragic. Remorse. Conscience. She's still full of it, so she gives it a last chance, driving crazy, lying dead together holding hands in the middle of the road, off together on an eternity kick. Twenty percent on a catch of three hundred and fifty thousand dollars' worth of gold, that's almost twice what Angel is paying. But it isn't the dough either, it's personal.

Slowing down for the frontier now. Hundred and ten. Ninety. Life again.

Well, that's how even the best things end.

Then she stopped the car. He took a deep breath and closed his eyes, smiling. Okay, kid, do it now. It's good for my philosophy.

He didn't see the guard come up, but he heard him all right.

– Will you step inside, please?

He looked up. Real innocent.

– Who, me?

– No, you, mademoiselle.

She gave him that good, cold, diplomat's daughter stare.

– This is a CC car. Here is my passport.

– Sorry, you'll have to discuss that with the chief.

She hesitated briefly, then stepped out of the car.

He watched her go, grinning. That's right, baby, go in there and see what you can do for me. But you know something? Nobody's going to catch me with my pants down. If you think you'll be locked up with me in the same cell for the rest of your sex life, you're dead wrong, let me tell you that.

There was only a thirty-yard walk to the guardroom and she had to think fast, as fast as she had ever thought in her life. They had no right to search the car without her permission. And it was unthinkable that the American Consulate should have canceled her diplomatic passport so brutally after her father's death and without notifying her. It had to be something else. As she walked into the office a man got up from the desk, the usual round, flabby, overfed French police type.

There was something vaguely familiar about him and then, as he walked toward her, his hand extended, she suddenly knew what it was: the feet. They were there on the night of the murder, the big, heavy, flat feet of plain reality.

– Good afternoon, Miss Donahue. I don't know if you remember me. You were in a state of shock. Please sit down.

– I'm in rather a hurry.

– I have something important to tell you and it may be a bit painful.

– I think I can take it standing, if you don't mind.

– As you wish.

He seemed genuinely embarrassed. He paced the floor, stopped by the window, looked gloomily at the Sunbeam, turned toward her again.

– I feel quite badly about it. Quite badly.

– May I ask you to tell me what it is you wish from me? The inspector sighed.

– You see, Miss Donahue, in a way I'm a little responsible for your father's death. We knew he had some financial difficulties . . . debts . . . personal problems and so forth. . . . Then, of course, we learned he had lost his official position. Well . . . we knew from different . . . complaints that he needed money rather badly. At one moment we approached him with a proposal, and . . . how shall I put it? You know perhaps there is a twenty percent reward on every contraband catch. He had agreed to help us.

She stood still for a moment, then she laughed. The inspector looked a bit pained. It was so close to the pure Swiss moral air that even the French police were getting easily shocked. She glanced through the window toward Lenny in the car. She laughed again. It was the funniest thing. Samson Delila and his Pussycats. Reality in full bloom. Her father acting as an informer for the French police. Lenny was dead right. It was the funniest thing, all of it. You had to laugh.

– Please go on, Inspector, I'm interested.

The inspector coughed.

– We were trying for months to break a smuggling ring dealing in gold. Millions and millions of dollars' worth of gold flee from the general political insecurity of the world into the safe refuge of Switzerland. Your father's financial difficulties were public knowledge and he was approached by one of the gangs. Diplomats often are. It's sometimes gold, sometimes heroin. At our suggestion he pretended to cooperate and . . .

– And they killed him.

The inspector nodded, then waited mournfully for her reaction. She smiled.

– You certainly picked the wrong man for the job, Inspector. He was very, very ineffectual in practical matters. In fact, the most ineffectual, unrealistic man I've ever known. . . .

Her voice shook a little and she almost broke down. The inspector looked pleased.

– We don't know at all what happened. We had taken all possible precautions. There was practically no risk involved at all. We knew the delivery point in Geneva, and we carefully, very carefully, set a . . . *souricière*, a mousetrap, as we call it, with the excellent cooperation of the Swiss authorities. But your father never turned up at the rendezvous. No one did. They seem to have suspected or discovered the part he was playing and they killed him, to avoid identification, I presume. But there's an element in it all that eludes us completely. We don't know what happened to the gold. As far as we know it is still on the French side, and they're probably looking for someone to take it over the border.

She glanced through the window again. He was sunning himself, his eyes closed, with a contented air. His blond hair was full of light. She was learning something now about moral overkill. It's painless and it leaves you incapable of any feeling and so capable of doing almost anything. It gives you that most vaunted contemporary value, total moral freedom. You could become a promiscuous bitch, or a heroin addict, or a thief, without the slightest feeling of remorse. You were set truly free at last. The only thing that was left to wonder about was why on earth they still bothered to build the Bomb.

– How perfectly fascinating, she said.

The inspector looked hurt again. Strong sense of moral values, or he wouldn't be in the police. I expect he'll tell me next he's got a daughter my age. There was a kind of what's-happening-to-our-kids air about him. She had never felt better in her whole life. She felt dead, in fact.

She sat down, crossed her nylons, took a cigarette from the pack on the table and lit it.

– Why are you telling me all this, Inspector? Are you working on my father's image for my benefit?

– Please, Miss Donahue, I know it's very painful. . . . I am telling you this because we are a bit concerned for your safety. You see, they wouldn't have searched your house the way they did after the murder if they had recovered the gold. They seem to have looked for it everywhere in a kind of blind panic, as if they didn't know where it was. . . .

The gold is in my car and one of the bastards who did it is in my car too, sunning himself. She could see him through the window, his eyes closed, his head resting lazily on the back of the seat, with a completely unconcerned, nonchalant air. Smiling, in fact. A blind faith in humanity, I suppose. He had put Sinatra's "The Lady Is a Tramp" on her record player and he was basking in the sun, waiting for her. I have only to say one word and he would spend a couple of years in jail, and I could always take a job in the same town so as to be close to him. She felt tempted. But then you can't turn informer and co-operate with the police when you still have some literary ambitions. She was going to do something much better than that.

– The chances are they may still be looking for it. They may think you know where it is. They might threaten you, or at least approach you about it. In this case ...

He cleared his throat and waited.

– I see. You have already managed to have my father killed. I'm glad to feel I can still be of some further use to you.

– We are only trying to find out who committed this abominable crime, Miss Donahue.

– And incidentally recover the gold.

– Incidentally, yes. If something turns up, I think you ought to warn us. Here is my card. You can reach me at this number at any time.

– But of course. It's only natural. The moment I have the slightest suspicion I'll remember the twenty percent reward.

She squashed her cigarette in the ashtray and walked back to the Sunbeam, got in behind the wheel and sat completely still for a few seconds, trying to survive. Come on, Jess, it's only the end of the world, happens all the time. All you have to do is not let yourself be buried under the moral debris. All right, so your father did end up as a police informer, why not, it was only an act of love. He wanted you to be rich, and you're going to be exactly that, five minutes from now, and it's going to be an act of love, too.

– What did they want?

– Nothing, he told me how sorry he was about my father.

– Angel swears he had nothing to do with it, you know. Must be another crowd.

– I don't care.

She started the car across the frontier. They were almost there. All I have to do now is to get out of sight of the Buick before I turn off the road.

– Hey, what's the big hurry now?

– I only want to get rid of you and your damn gold and get paid.

– There ain't no gold in this car, kid.

She stepped on the brakes so hard they were almost thrown off the road. He was grinning his best. Freckles, too. I suppose you can be a bastard and still have freckles.

– They were only feeling you out to see if you were playing it straight. I told them you were, but they're not taking any chances. It's only natural. Hey, don't give me that pure hate look, they had to make sure somehow, didn't they?

As a matter of fact, so had I.

– Come on, kid, you can love me tender, but you don't have to hate me just because you don't like me, okay?

– Now what?

– Nothing, you turn back and we go it again. For real, this time. Same place. Half an hour from now, okay?

– I'll want my twelve thousand dollars, cash and in advance before we cross the frontier.

– They'll have to go to Geneva for that.

– I don't care.

– Give it an hour then.

He got out of the car and took the suitcase and sat by the hedge at the side of the road, waiting for Angel to pick him up. He crossed his arms over his knees and buried his face there. He had never felt so close to giving up something, he didn't even know what. There must be one billion guys on earth and all and each of them live without her, so why couldn't I? Except that I can't. She's gone subliminal on me. Life propaganda's set in. Love. Happiness. Something to live for. Jesus Christ, I've got to get my principles back. I'm going to grab my twelve thousand bucks and run away to Euthanasia, I bet they've got good eternal snow there.

Except, Jesus, there's just nothing I can do without her that can be called living.

She drove back and waited in the field under the Cinzano sign and this time there were three other guys in the back of the Buick when it came up behind her, and then, when Lenny jumped in beside her she knew this was it. He wasn't even pretending any longer, no more bragging, he was all funk, and it made her feel good and calm.

– Why are you so scared?

– Why? What d'you mean, why? It's the first time in my life I'm trusting someone or something. How d'you want me to feel? Suppose you turn me in to the police? What happens to us then?

He meant it, too. A guy is okay, he has made it, he's got detachment and futility, and then a thing like that hits him and shakes up everything he doesn't believe in and you get all screwed up inside and you don't mind a bit giving up everything you don't believe in and go for everything you don't believe in either, and then you don't know, you just don't know any more. With twenty-four thousand bucks between us we could make it somehow, one way or another.

– What you waiting for?

– Where are my twelve thousand?

He grabbed the envelope in his pocket and threw it on her lap. She opened it calmly and began to count the bills. He looked back, he could almost feel Angel drilling into him. Right behind. The other guys looked mean too.

– Listen, they aren't going to cheat you on that, this is too big. There must be half a million worth of gold in that suitcase.

She felt quite thrilled. Half a million worth of reality. Now we're getting somewhere at last.

She started the car.

The Buick kept close behind, but there was no problem there, she had found that out on the first run. Three minutes' margin was more than enough. And the kids were straight out from their army training, if it came to the worst. The Swiss citizens keep their individual army weapons at home, it goes back to the beginning of Swiss democracy. She didn't drive fast. The first run had taken care of her nerves.

Jesus Christ. His back was covered in cold sweat and his ass was glued to the seat. He still tried to make a good job of it, a real who-cares Lenny face, and it's true, too, who cares, it's worth spending a year in jail to get rid of her and to know for sure and get your principles and lucidity back so that life can't get sweet and important on you again. Except he was so scared to find out that he wished he was dead, then you can keep your illusions intact.

Then he saw the frontier ahead and got goose pimples and she slowed down and stopped and looked at him.

He sat there with his eyes closed, holding his breath, and his face was so pathetic with something that wasn't even funk she had to look away.

I shouldn't have looked at him. I have to do everything the hard way. He's so scared it can't be funk alone.

Holy Moses, Holy Moses. I have never prayed before in

my life, so it means something this time, honestly it does.

She glanced at him again. He had dug both his hands deep into his pockets, his eyes still closed. I bet he's holding a rabbit's foot in his pocket.

Jesus.

Then he felt the car jerk forward and he opened his eyes. They were through. Only it was different this time. It felt so good it was like nothing he had ever known. Happiness, that's what it was. It sure took care of your principles for you. He felt like kissing her, like singing, like shouting, I love you, Jess, I love you. He had to face it somehow, it was the worst thing that had ever hit him. It was all making sense and falling into place around you, and life was looking so beautiful all of a sudden it scared the shit out of him. What next? God? Yes, you can say that, I guess. You could start believing in almost anything now, that's how bad it was. I love you, Jess. Except that you couldn't say a thing like that. It was bad for virility.

– You know, Jess, I respect you for going through with this, no kidding. You sure know what it's all about.

Bragging again, thank God. It helps.

She was driving crazy again. He didn't feel like getting killed at all now, that's how good he felt.

They had about five minutes' advance on the Buick now. She slowed down a bit. Now.

An accident, he thought, she had lost control. He tried to grab the steering wheel, but then the Sunbeam swayed off the road so suddenly he was thrown right and left and forward and he tried to hold on to the door, and then the car was jumping mad for a few crazy seconds between trees too, faster and faster, and then he got the windshield smack into his face, real hard, and he heard the brakes, then silence, and all he could think of at first was his ass, how come it's still there, and then he saw some Swiss Army guys in uniform and one of them was pointing his rifle at him. He sat there dead for a moment, then lucidity set in. He glanced at Jess and she turned her head away at once, like when you see blood, so he just knew.

That kid was the best thing that had ever hit him. There's nothing like getting first-hand information when you're only twenty-one. You need the experience, it's good for maturity. They're sure right when they say you haven't lived if you haven't loved.

– Thanks, kid.

Right from the diaphragm. He meant it, too. She was still looking away like mad. Sensitive bitch.

– Get out.

That was the guy with the horn-rimmed glasses over his ass face. There were other guys around, all armed, and even a nigger. What next? He didn't know they had that in Switzerland too. I hope they get the problem, the lousy bastards. There were also two twins, and they all liked him, he could tell that, but not quite the way the fellow with the glasses liked him. You could tell it was personal, the way he was pressing the rifle against his chest. Strictly personal. Well, I seem to have quite a reputation around here, so let's build it up.

– Why you so mad at me, lover boy? It was only sex.

– Get out, you bastard.

He got out, nice and all, he didn't even feel like being killed, that's how good he felt again. Now that nothing made sense again, it was all making sense once more. There's just nothing like not being confused any longer.

He took another look around, just for curiosity. They were in uniform all right, the whole lousy bunch of them, except there was a nineteen-thirty yellow Packard and a green Baby Austin there and that's not what the Swiss Army goes driving around in. So it was all personal, all of it. They sure loved him here.

There was another guy coming up at him with a thermos flask. Nice guy, all shook up. You could get sympathy there.

– D-drink that.

Why not? Let's get rid of the bastard. She was still scared to look at him, that's how sensitive she was. Couldn't hurt a fly.

He took a gulp. Good coffee. Hot. No sugar, but then thanks, I had about all the sugar I can take.

– What's in there for me, fellow? Arsenic?

—H-hurry up. It's only d-d-dope.

He drank some more. He liked the idea, sort of. Anastasia. He could do with a lot of that. You could feel the guy with the thermos flask was sorry for him. Soft.

He wished she would look at him, though. Just once, for heartbreak. He had the right kind of face for her now. He was a natural for that.

– I'm going to say one thing for you, Jess.

He waited a moment, for suspense.

– You're the best lay I ever had.

That did it. The lover boy with glasses let him have it with the butt of his rifle, a fast one on the back of the head, true army stuff, like Algeria, then another and another, and my! did that help. Good solid, physical pain, it's the best there is to take your mind off the real thing. He came down. But he was still around, you just couldn't get rid of the bastard. He tried to turn his head toward her, but couldn't make it, I bet she's still looking away, protecting herself. Then the stuff began to work almost at once and he lay flat on his back, sunny side up. Anastasia. I bet she isn't doing this for money, she does this for love. It's personal. She really has it for me, I guess. He could hear them talking, far away someplace.

– Don't panic now, Jess, he'll be all right. . . .

– It's only d-dope. . . .

The sky was all over him, doing its bit, blue and all, full of propaganda. *Who took the cookie from the cookie jar?* I guess it was never there at all. He liked the blue of it, though. I bet it can get you subliminal. They must sell a lot of that. He was beginning to feel Anastasia in his blood and in his eyes now, but kept looking at the sky some more, just for the blue of it. *Drink that, it's only dope. Thirst drunk.* I wonder what that Dominican son of a bitch meant by that. *Thirst drunk.* Aw, propaganda. You sure can't get any protection here, except when you're a dog, then you can go to the SPCA and get humanity. *Who took the cookie from the cookie jar? Not I took the cookie from the cookie jar. . . . Then who . . .* Then he began to fall and spin around, and just when he was getting rid of the bastard at last he felt such a bite of loneliness and longing for something or someone he kicked his eyes wide open again and looked up there with everything he had and did his best, his very best, but all he could come up with was Gary Cooper.

When he came round she was driving.

At first he thought it was only a nightmare and he closed his eyes, reassured, and settled back to sleep it out, but then he jumped up screaming and it was her all right, driving, and it scared him so bad he yelled, Jesus, help, the way she had been driving on that road it had to happen, they had crashed into that tree just as he thought they would, they were out on an eternity kick now, he was really stuck with her, and he felt his hair stand on end the way they say it does, and he yelled, what the hell is going on here, where are we, and she said Italy, and he glanced around, mountains, it was dark, and he made for the door shouting, let me out of here, but she only drove a little faster and he said meekly, Jesus, let me out of here, please, please, but she only smiled and there was even the moon

out and he just didn't know any more, he didn't know at
all, except that it was summer all right, the worst thing that
can hit a guy, he had always said that.

– What happened?

– I love you, Lenny.

It made no sense at all, so he couldn't be dreaming.

Italy, what d'you know.

Oh, well, I don't speak the language, so I guess I'll be
okay.

Then his head cleared some more and it all came back
to him and he felt indignant and started to yell again but
she just put one hand over his, gently but firmly, be a good
boy, sort of, maternity, so he shut up, he wasn't going to
take any more chances with that bitch.

– I can't live without you, Lenny.

If only she'd slow down a bit, he could jump out and
run and hide with some kind, fine people, the summer was
almost over, maybe he could still make it somehow. Except
that he didn't feel like it at all, he didn't even mind, so it's
the end, I guess.

He was a broken man, that's what he was.

Italy.

The moon.

It's murder.

– I love you with all my heart, Lenny.

Sounded like something from outer space, so maybe it
was true. It always comes from outer space, they say. Bits of
it. Particles. Cosmic dust. It's got to be cosmic, there isn't

any of that on earth, they don't make it here. But there must be a lot of it where it comes from. It can't come from nowhere, science says so, there's got to be a source. And it must be reaching the earth now, or she wouldn't be here, looking at him, her eyes full of tears as though she really meant it.

It's got to come from somewhere, Jesus Christ.

A source. It's scientific.

It might still take a million years for the real thing to reach the earth, you've got to be patient, but it's on its way here all right and some of it is beginning to bless you even though you could do with a lot more of the same.

Particles.

I can feel them right here in my diaphragm, too. Warm and glowing. It's got to be cosmic and it takes awful long to travel, but that's what science always said, they don't go by time up there, they don't have the same measurements.

– I can't live without you, Lenny.

– Okay, but where do I come in?

– Please, don't be scared. We'll make it somehow.

Some somehow. But then he could feel the particles glowing inside him and they couldn't come out of nowhere, science says so. You can't fight science, there's just too much of it.

A lot of it gets lost on the way and it reaches you small and human, sort of, but it's got to be big where it starts from.

There's got to be a source.

Love. What d'you know. It doesn't travel fast enough, though. What it sure needs is transportation.

His head was full of jangling stones, he couldn't move his neck, his tongue was made of lead, one of his eyes felt twice the size of the other, but he didn't mind and he even began to grin, all of a sudden. It was still better than nothing.

– How come it's you and me here?

– I simply couldn't do it, that's all.

He gave up. He'd been feeling like giving up for a long, long time. I guess it's maturity, they say it always gets you in the end. I don't seem to have any more principles left, so it's got to be maturity.

– What are we going to do for a living?

– We've still got the twelve thousand you gave me.

That's right, he thought. Security. What next? It made sense, though, so maybe it's only dope. He still felt a bit dopy, so that must be it. Italy. Security. Particles. I don't mind any more. Giving up, I mean. I guess it's part of it. You've got to give up, that's known as maturity.

– I love you too, Jess.

It was his voice, all right. Must be the dope. It shook him hard to hear himself saying a thing like that, and in Italy too. It shook him so hard he felt a broken man again. He even took her hand and held it and his throat was full and it was creeping up into his eyes too. Physiology, you have no control over that. A broken man, I guess that's what you become, the moment you're no longer a kid. And the worst part was that he had never felt better in his life, that's how bad it was.

– Where's the gold?

– They'll give it to the police.

Criminals. But then to hell with it, he had about all he could take from principles. She was sobbing like mad now.

– What's the matter, Jess? Don't take it so hard, kid. Maybe we'll make it somehow.

– It's not that. I've got something awful to tell you.

Jesus, so that's what it is. I thought it was only me.

– You pregnant?

– Oh no, nothing like that.

So it's still okay, it's still only me. He felt so detached and cool he could go and marry her tomorrow, that's how little he cared now. He just didn't give a damn.

– What is it, then?

– I came back for you. We took the suitcase and I left you lying there. It almost killed me but I did it.

You bitch. He felt hurt. But you can't have it perfect, not all the time.

– What next?

– We had planned to take the gold directly to the bank, put it in a safe deposit box there. My father had a box and I had a key. So we drove to the bank and went in with the suitcase and opened the box. . . .

She started to sob again. Hysterics. He put an arm around her for virility.

– And there it was.

– There was what?

– The gold.

Jesus Christ.

– What gold?

– The other gold.

Made no sense at all, except that it sure seems to be lying around everywhere.

– I don't get it.

– It was another crowd, Lenny. My father had gone along with another crowd and then he kept the money and they killed him. You had nothing to do with it. I always knew that, believe me.

Yeah. But as the Chinese cookie said, you can't have it perfect. It was a nice drive anyway. Moonshine. Money. Particles. You can't have it perfect. That's known as maturity.

– I still don't get it.

– My father was broke and he had agreed to work for the police and he offered to smuggle the gold in on his CC plates, just as I did, but then all he wanted all the time was to get hold of the money . . . for me.

Hysterics again.

– You better watch your driving, kid.

He didn't feel like going on an eternity kick any longer. You've got to learn how to give up. He touched her neck and her hair. The softest neck and the softest hair. It ought to do. Particles. You may as well settle for that.

– They killed him, as he knew they would. He loved me.

Some particles, though. The things people do for their kids. Crazy. Maybe I'm going to try it someday myself. There must be something in it.

– What happened to that other dough?

You've got to be practical, what the hell. I've got a wife and kids now.

– They'll give it back too.

Sick, that's what it was. Sick. Going socialist like that. Oh well. Maybe there'll be another chance. There always is. He had never felt so optimistic in his whole life. That's one thing dope can do for you.

– I know you had nothing to do with it, Lenny. I always knew that. You must believe me. . . .

He grinned and pressed his arm around her a little tighter for tolerance.

– It's okay, kid. No harm.

– So I jumped into my car and rushed back and . . .

And. Some and. He was beginning to feel sleepy again. But then you go to sleep and the next thing you know you wake up and find out you were only dreaming. So he tried to keep his eyes open. He didn't feel like waking up at all.

– The things people do for their kids. Must be something in it.

She was quiet now. Just sniffling a bit. He still kept his arm around her. Such a clear night too. Beautiful, yeah, you could almost say that, beautiful. Italy, what d'you know? They sing there. His eyelids felt so heavy he just couldn't fight it any more. He had to trust it. Maybe he would wake up and find it still all there. All of it. Particles. Italy. The moon. The warm, soft neck under his hand and the hand on his cheek. Even the twelve thousand bucks. Why not? There's even a Chinese cookie for it, a *sukiyaki* or a *koulebiaki* or whatever those oriental pearls of wisdom are called: you've got to trust someone or something, that's known as living. There's a Chinese cookie for everything.

Format by Gayle Jaeger
Set in Granjon
HARPER & ROW, PUBLISHERS, INCORPORATED